RISE OF THE UNICORN
by
D. ELLIOT WOODS

Table of Contents

Prologue.. 1
Chapter 1... 5
Chapter 2...17
Chapter 3...25
Chapter 4...33
Chapter 5...41
Chapter 6...49
Chapter 7...57
Chapter 8...67
Chapter 9...75
Chapter 10 83
Chapter 11 91
Chapter 12 97
Chapter 13 105
Chapter 14 115
Chapter 15 123
Chapter 16 131
Chapter 17 139
Chapter 18 147
Chapter 19 153
Chapter 20 165
Epilogue.. 167

• • • •

• • • •

PAPERBACK ISBN: 979-8-9867-6150-3[3]
E-book ISBN: 979-8-9867-6152-7

---

1.   http://www.FlyFreeEnt.com

2.   http://www.FlyFreeEnt.com

3. https://www.myidentifiers.com/title_registration?isbn=979-8-9867615-0-3&icon_type=Assigned

For Sydney, Maya, Denis II and Verdel. Three plus a bonus... who <u>always</u> make me proud.

RISE OF THE UNICORN

FOREWORD

My name is Robb Armstrong.

I am the creator of the nationally syndicated comic strip, "JumpStart".

I am also Executive Producer of the CBS sitcom of the same name. I'm a screenwriter, speaker, and author as well.

My most relevant credential is this: I'm best friends with D. Elliot Woods. *

There is an asterisk for a reason. Lots of men and women in LA make this claim.

The author of "RISE OF THE UNICORN" surrounds himself with people who genuinely love him.

When they see that my claim is established here in black and white, I'm pretty sure there will be hell to pay.

Elliot's humorous demeanor and charming wit are not solely responsible for his popularity.

Simply put, he possesses the rare ability to dispense advice and wisdom without a trace of judgement.

And it seems effortless.

I happen to know, by way of our friendship of more than a decade, that there is more underneath. Like all of us, Elliot has experienced his share of pain and challenges. In many ways, it fuels him. When he advises me, he is actually advising himself, so it feels soothing.

Our journey as best friends has many twists and turns, but one worth mentioning here is the time we appeared on a television show together. OWN network's "Home Made Simple" had us playing best friends (what a stretch), while the author had a room remodeled by the staff and hostess of the show, Laila Ali. Yep. The former boxing world champion, daughter of Muhammad Ali and... new friend of Elliot's.

It was on the set of this reality show that I first heard the bare bones description of the book you are about to read. It was a bustling set, and I must confess that when Elliot began telling me about it, I thought he was telling an actual story involving people he knew! I interrupted him more than once to say, "Is this for real?"

This is the mark of gripping, authentic fiction: characters whom you believe are living souls.

I hope Elliot hurries up and completes the audiobook for this title, as he is an excellent actor. I was on the edge of my folded seat as his heist concept was being acted out for me while the author sipped water and honey. (He swears by the soothing properties of a long list of lozenges, lollipops and other honey-based throat remedies). I realized that the characters in his book idea were amalgams of Elliot, as he has had an inordinate amount of experience with the U.S. Court System. Even others who know him might find this fact surprising. This book's concept was a personal reckoning and a societal query. Indeed. 'What is more valuable than money?'

Elliot had his whole family on set that day, and they each had camera time. He would spend time with his three children- the youngest, a daughter, his constantly growing son, his teenage daughter, and, of course, his mom (aka Nana-Betts), then turn into "Gus" or "Jones" while describing his book idea to me. It was a stunning impromptu performance from my friend.

It is a marvel to hold in my hands the finished product from that fascinating day. The show turned out pretty good, too. It was a joy to work professionally with my friend. I treasure the lived experience because it has affected the way I approach characters in my writing. I work hard to make my characters resonate with authenticity the way the characters do in "RISE OF THE UNICORN".

I believe that D. Elliot Woods has penned a modern masterpiece.

He has trusted his characters and believed in their realness. From the first page to the last, you will hold onto them for dear life and, quite possibly come away a changed person-which of course, is the true purpose for an artist.

Happy reading...

-Robb Armstrong. Creator of "JumpStart"

4:44 am in white digital clock font stared back in silence.

According to an affirmation book she'd scanned through at some point, whenever one glanced at the time on a clock, and it displayed repetitive numbers, that person should give thanks to God for all the things in their life they were grateful for.

And there was a lot to be grateful for, but what Evelyn Kennedy, aka 'Lynn,' really wanted was to simply be able to sleep until her alarm went off. Instead, she consistently woke up 45 minutes or so prior, with her mind racing about past, present, and future matters, issues, and circumstances. So, rather than the restful sleep she yearned for, Lynn's habit was to sort through all of – what her mother had called her 'mind mess material' - by making mental lists by category and level of priority.

All of it.

Every morning.

Everyone in her inner circle knew that her relationship with her late mother had been complicated, to say the least. But besides the eternal necessity to organize her mind mess, one of the many things drilled into her mind and spirit from as far back as she could remember was that she always needed to be "twice as good, to get half as much."

Anything less simply would not suffice under her mom's ever watchful and judgmental eye.

While one part of her brain prioritized the mind mess, another part multitasked and allowed her to reflect on mostly pleasant memories and simpler times while she slowly and soothingly slid her feet back and forth over the twelve hundred thread-count sheets she allowed herself as a reward and a reminder.

Pleasures could be given or received, but luxuries, for her, were earned.

Job promotions were also earned, but the terms are often nebulous or coded in ways that leave both the uninitiated and the unacceptable on the outside grasping at hope-filled balloons to assist in the process of attaining the invisible. People in this category unknowingly seek to be awarded for playing nice and checking all the little metaphorical boxes companies and organizations like to see.

Lynn's promotion had come about because of meticulous planning, making her 'outside the box' thinking appear 'in the box' to casual observers as well as habitual under-estimators and, of course, the willful intention of playing 3-dimensional chess while never acknowledging the game. No, her job promotion was not an award; it was a reward because ... ...

"Twice as good" was her minimum standard.

Evelyn Kennedy had become the first African American woman to obtain the title of LAPD Commissioner almost one month ago to the day.

Indeed, there was much to be grateful for. Life was 'good' but she didn't allow herself to indulge her ego because she understood that the work still needed to be done. The department and its members were not exactly 'on board' yet because she'd been appointed by an embattled Mayor who some accused of scoring political points by his use of the diversity wild card, which was the equivalent of silently and unexpectedly throwing down the 'big' joker to quiet the loud voices at the Spades table. So, without question, a significant percentage of the over ten thousand cops, in her new department maintained a degree of skepticism regarding her qualifications and capabilities. Add to that the fact she'd come from outside the department, and... because she was who and what she was, one could conclude that she'd been set up to fail or distract from someone else's political problems.

'But good things come to she who waits,' she thought confidently while smiling in the still dark bedroom. What Evelyn Kennedy didn't know was that the first real test of her mettle as Police Commissioner would come later that same day – under the glare of the brightest of spotlights.

It was then that Drew rolled over in his sleep and put his arm around her, pulling her close. This unexpected but welcome surprise caused Lynn to put a hold on organizing her mind mess because giving and receiving pleasure for a recently relocated husband and wife team was suddenly a priority and would soon provide a reward they'd both earn.

The glow from this early morning dalliance will need to sustain her because her multi-level chess-playing capabilities would soon be stress-tested beyond anything she's ever experienced or imagined.

And many lives will surely swing in the balance while the world watches because, literally one month after being named Police Commissioner of the LAPD, the events of today will either become one of her most accomplished memories, or it will be the absolute worst day of Lynn Kennedy's professional life.

Chapter 1

U nicorn: **A mythical creature that seeks purity and light and has the power to heal.**

· · · ·

SUN VALLEY, CALIFORNIA, is six miles away from the suburban outskirts of Los Angeles, but the tangible look and texture of the area are so different, in a myriad of ways, from its larger and more well-known first cousin that any outsider would no doubt believe L. A was hundreds, if not thousands, of miles away.

It was early morning - too early to be making so much noise. The sun hadn't come up, and the neighbors were certainly not pleased.

Generically speaking, this was a domestic violence call, but there were many other components like 240 assault, 242 battery, 390 intoxicated people... it was your basic 'hot mess.'

Typically, it had all started with an argument about something unmemorable that rose in decibel levels to the point of yelling until the stomach-sickening thudding sounds of physical violence inevitably began. Those sounds gave birth to the muffled, inarticulate screams that accompany ferocious struggle when the line between love and hate becomes invisible – assuming love was ever present to begin with. Then, apparently, came what sounded like a gunshot. Even worse on an otherwise quiet night in a town like this was the silence piercing wail of multiple police sirens announcing the situation like roosters that hate the impending sunrise.

Now, adding insult to injury was a drone buzzing forth and back over the street. More noise, more god-awful noise robbing people in the vicinity of this disturbance of their final precious winks of sleep or the last blissful minutes of good, old-fashioned quiet.

Emergency vehicles were stationed all along the street. Indeed, the whole road was blocked off. The police were running a major op in the not-so-nice apartments within one of several 'icky' parts of town.

One window out of all the rest had its lights on the entire night, and any view into that window was blocked by a dingy, rotting, beige curtain that had come with this sadly furnished rental unit.

This was the small living room of a couple who bickered constantly and were now in the middle of yet another fight that brought in a certain someone who'd gotten the call to come to settle things.

The team listened in from the safety of their vehicles out front.

"For Thanksgiving?" a woman asked. Her voice was shaky and worn out from the previous night. She was on guard, and her voice slowly grew softer. "I... I don't know. Uh, turkey, I guess. The dark meat... with gravy if it's good."

"That's the gospel truth," a man replied.

He was their man on the inside. Special operations and tactical takedowns. Their negotiator.

"If the gravy ain't right, don't much else matter. My favorite part? Rum cake. Yeah, my momma's rum cake ties everything together. That's when it feels like home for me."

Augustus Martin, aka Gus, was crouched low outside of the apartment's front door in a bulletproof vest, labeled 'POLICE', along with a small team of police officers who held positions against the interior hallway wall on the 3rd floor.

Gus wasn't as hardened nor as armed as the others. He'd arrived wearing a collared shirt underneath, not a tactical coat or even a deep blue button-down. He had on California Casual slacks, an odd-looking pullover, and unimpressive tennis shoes. Although handsome under all his eccentricities, he appeared to be a rather average black man beneath his Kevlar vest. To be honest, he was unshaven, decidedly unfashionable, and a tad unkempt.

During the lapses in conversation, Gus consulted with the digital screen at his side. He worked the antiquated past-generation drone controls until the thing finally leveled out outside the window of the living room, behind the door he was facing. He angled the thing and its camera around in a wide sweep that nearly took it into the side of a similarly unspectacular building next door. He could not get a complete view of their apartment interior. The woman he'd been talking to wasn't visible. Neither was the child she allegedly was holding a gun on.

There was, obviously, a man in there too. His shadow and part of his swaying upper torso could be seen intermittently cast against a wall on the right side of the screen but to Gus' actual left as he faced the front door. Gus could see the standoff was set to continue, the man with what looked to be a belt wrapped around his fist and the other two, perhaps better armed but clearly hiding for a reason.

"I done told you." the man inside shouted. "You get that off-a him! I ain't gon' bother you -"

"-RAY?" Gus loudly reminded. "I asked you to stay quiet."

Even from the other side of the door, he commanded the situation. Ray stuttered a bit but reluctantly went silent. Gus' tone was agreeable, accommodating even. Not risen in anger, just to be heard. Gus was part of their conversation, of what was happening. He was there, which meant no one could make any decisions without consulting him. He was the moderate messenger and the angel of mercy who carried a sword to fight evil, and he was on her side.

"Arlene? How ya coming? I want to help you, and everybody get through this so-" Gus said.

"No! You stop trying to handle me!" she shouted.

The officers got unsettled. Gus held his hand up gently to stop them from acting impulsively.

"You all show up now. Finally! Where was you when I needed help? I told y'all I needed me a restraining order on him three times!

Three different times! Ain't nobody do nothin!' Telling me, he had to commit something first - even though I told y'all what he was!" Arlene clamored.

"Arlene?" Gus said. "I understand. I'm sorry the Police couldn't get you what you needed when you needed it. Restraining orders can be tricky – trickier than they need to be."

He spoke with a heavier air of honesty than any polite acting pretense could ever command.

"But if you really want him to pay, you gotta know, this—this won't get you what you want," Gus said.

He was interrupted by a buzz in his pocket. He pulled out his cellphone. It was a direct line with the captain, who was texting from downstairs outside.

'Move subject to her right and cause to stand. Positioning shooter now.'

He glowered at the message. He was making significant progress, but the detailed explanation as to why and how wasn't something he could put into 280 characters or less. The door was still between them, and that barrier needed to come down; with words.

"Gotdamn right, he's gonna suffer!" Arlene shouted. "After what he done!"

"Arlene?" Gus called out. "You gotta let us take care of it. You don't want to hurt anybody. Justin's a good kid, right? Not his fault he's Ray's son. He's not Ray. Look, you gotta think this thing through."

"I ain't force her daughter to do shit!" Ray interjected. "Y'all get in here and shoot this stupid cunt!"

"Shut up, Ray!" Gus said with some frustration. Clearly, the boys outside were looking for the wrong target. He brought his phone up close to his mouth, turned away from the door, and whispered. "No, period. Hold shot, period. Going in, period." The auto-text completed his order perfectly. He sent it, pocketed the phone, and then quickly

8

kissed the pendant attached to the gold chain around his neck before putting it back under his shirt.

"Arlene?" Gus asked. "I have to come in there. My boss said I need to assess the situation, and she's on my ass. Now, I know how you feel, but she's making me, and well, she's in charge. I do not have any weapons on me. I promise. Is it okay with you if I come in?"

Arlene stuttered. "No, you stay on out there! I just need to think for a minute!"

"Bitch, that's 55 seconds more'n you can handle!" Ray said.

Ray was getting in the way, and Gus couldn't shut him up through the wall.

"ARLENE!" Gus called out. He could tell just how finely she was being pulled. He had to get through to her and be a louder, more insistent voice than the one that habitually sank the deepest into her. "I see what you mean about Ray. He is a pain in the ass! I'm sick of listening to him myself. How about I come in there, and I make him shut up?"

Ray got insulted. "Me? She's the fuckin' problem. You get in here and do your goddamn job!"

Gus signaled to the officers in the hall to stay. They turned to one another and nodded in agreement. He handed off the drone cam to one of them and his clip-on holster to another. He prepared to go in unarmed, as promised. There was a silent, visual rejection from the officer who took his gun. Gus gave him a reassuring nod as he reached to open the door. He got maybe an inch of clearance before the security chain tugged the door to a complete stop. He could barely see inside the living room. Arlene was still nowhere in his line of sight, but she had to be on his right. Ray was on the far-left side, just a slip of a shadow rocking back and forth against the far wall.

"Arlene," Gus began quieter and much clearer through the opening. "Think now... Thanksgiving's gonna come around. Who's gonna help your daughter if we don't handle this the right way? Who's gonna help Stacey, Arlene?"

He waited. He heard her breath shudder as her rage turned to tears. But the rage was still there. The gun cocked. "Don't you panic on me, Arlene. I'm gonna pop this door, and then I'm gonna come in - by myself. No weapon. I want to help you help Stacey, Arlene. Just me by myself... moving real slow."

Gus wound himself back and hit their door on the edge with as much of the vest on his shoulder as he could. More of a back tackle than a whole shoulder pivot. He only needed to snap the chain, not break the door. On the second strike, the flimsy chain slipped off the frame of the door. The door was open. He stopped it from swinging wide and carefully and deliberately stepped into the living room.

"Well, look at that," Ray semi-slurred, up against the wall. "They sent a nigger." That last part was crisp as a fresh apple. Because, of course, it was.

Ignoring Ray completely, Gus quickly surveyed the area of the Bradley-Nelson home. Arlene Nelson was in the far-right corner, behind a couch, with Justin Bradley in front of her as she held a gun to his head. She had a swollen left eye and assorted bruises along her arms. Her face was red with tears and the huffing breaths of rage she was still taking.

Justin, just ten years old or so, sat perfectly still and stared across the room at his father with eyes that come with a hard life. Even held up and one errant twitch away from death, his vacant eyes didn't show any fear or contempt. He was just stuck there, waiting for a conclusion he'd already accepted.

Saving the walking stereotype for last, Ray Bradley was exactly the sort Gus pictured from the outset, without needing to see a police profile. He was out of shape, out of luck, and out of his prime. Next to him, a broken picture frame on the wall held a different Ray from a lifetime ago as he sat, three over, on the front bench for the

Montgomery Biscuits AA baseball team. This minor league photo painted a pale comparison between the man Ray'd been trying to be and the one he became. Now both were, apparently, still drunk. The invisible accomplice, maybe the active accessory, was present only in the sour smell of the room.

Gus eyed the window directly across from where he stood. He saw reflections of the lights flashing from below outside and the low light of the sun rising to drown them out. He eyed the covered glass with worry. One window was exposed, the one his drone saw through. The one everyone was probably looking through the whole time. He kept his fears internal. He'd come in with a half-cocked relaxing smile and kept it even as he turned to Arlene.

"How we doing, Arlene? I'm Gus. Guess you know that. Captain thought it'd be better if we were all in the same room. No gun like I promised. Just me." He turned and fully faced her, then gave her a slow side view, just to be sure.

"You bein' in here don't change nothin'," she declared. "It ain't gonna undo what he has done to me... to my baby."

She was talking with certainty but much less of it from when they started. She wasn't aware of it, but through two hours of talking, Gus had worn her down with honesty and empathy. She didn't turn the gun on him or re-aim it because she trusted him. Still, she was speaking with a sad sense of finality. Like she was glad to see him, so she could threaten him to his face.

"You're right, Arlene," Gus agreed. "Me being here won't fix what Ray's done. You've had a rough go. I can see that. I came in here because my boss told me to help Stacey."

Arlene broke a little and opened up. "Why ain't they believe me when I told 'em what he was?"

Gus shook his head disappointingly. "Wish I had an answer that'd make sense, Arlene. Messed up as it is, sometimes the law just moves too slow."

"Sometimes the law just moves too slow," Ray said, mocking Gus with an over-affected accent that was somehow worse than his own. "That all you got? That's you working your magic? You make that bitch put that pistol down, and you do it now!"

Gus ignored Ray, very frankly. He spoke as soon as the last words left Ray's mouth like they were nothing more than a rattle from the community coin-operated washing machine down the hall.

"Toughest thing about my wife leaving me, Arlene," Gus began, "was me having to admit that I'd picked 'wrong.' She needed fixin', and I thought I could do it. What I didn't know was that I was broken too. And who really needed fixing was me. Hardest part? On some level, I thought all that foolishness was what I deserved."

Arlene paused. She held her position, but her intention softened up. Her arm was still aiming the gun at Justin's head, like she'd sat all the way back on her knees with her legs in a crooked fashion. She was listening to him. The tide had turned, however slightly, in Gus' favor.

"Now here you are, beat on and dragged in the mud because you thought you could put polish on a turd and make it shine. Didn't you, Arlene?" Gus said.

"The fuck is this?!?" Ray exclaimed. "Shoot her, you stupid fuck!"

Arlene tensed up.

Now, because of Ray, they all had to go two steps back. Gus decided to turn and face Ray for the first time, giving him the attention, he sought. And Ray didn't seem to appreciate it. Gus strode toward him, slowly – walking right past the window.

"The thing is," he continued, still speaking to Arlene with his back almost entirely to her, "Ray's always hated you, Arlene. He knew you could've done better if you ever chose to. So, this - this 'tough guy' beat you down, kept apologizing and doing it again until he finally decided he'd start in on your daughter. He pretended to be a big man even though he was just... this. See, if he ever let up, he knew you, and that boy there would see he wasn't shit. Look at him..."

He was right up to Ray. Ray pressed his back to the wall and gripped the belt in his hand - hard.

"Got a weapon in his hand and me in his face, but you know what, Arlene? He won't do anything cuz he knows I can see him for what he is." Gus' eyes focused and locked onto Ray's. "Isn't that, right?" He asked.

Gus could see Ray think about how much of a swing he could wind up with his arm pressed to the wall. His grip hardened. The leather in his hand creaked.

"You might want to drop that strap," Gus said, low and quiet. "I'm feeling threatened."

Ray did the math, then grimaced before dropping the belt.

"Face the wall," Gus commanded. Gus put his hand behind his back and pointed for Arlene to see his back pocket where his handcuffs were. Meanwhile, Ray turned around slowly, pretending he was choosing to do it. Once his front was to the wall, Gus slipped out the handcuffs and applied them to Ray's wrists behind his waist.

"The fuck are you cuffing me for?" Ray exclaimed. "That bitch has a gun at my -."

"No, she doesn't, Ray," Gus interrupted. "Way I see it, she's pointing the gun at you and protecting herself. 'Cuz, you kept beating on her and because of what you did to her daughter."

"Fuck you, nigger," Ray spat.

Gus lowered his voice, very personally. "Guess what, Ray? Soon, some of the brothas are gonna be fuckin' you. Won't that be something?"

Now that got Ray to quiet down, albeit impolitely. He tugged at the handcuffs reflexively while Gus gently held him in place. He turned back to Arlene.

"Since your gun there was for self-defense, maybe you don't need it now, and you can hand it over to me. That okay with you, Arlene?"

Arlene's hand that gripped Justin's shoulder gave out more than it let go. Her other hand dropped, gun still in it, but the weight was too much to hold up any longer. The subconscious relief she now felt caused her to fall. Justin turned to try and catch her and slowed her descent as the hours of tension broke her open like a leaky, tear-filled watermelon. "I'm sorry," she wept. "I didn't mean to -."

"It's okay," Justin said. "I knew you wouldn't hurt me."

Gus almost smiled. Everything seemed clear. He left Ray in place. He wouldn't do much more harm with his hands bound and his mind thoroughly occupied with the consequences of his many actions.

Gus started slow-walking back across the room to get the gun. Arlene stood up with the gun extended so she could meet him halfway there.

In front of the window.

Gus glanced outside. For a hot second, he thought he saw something across the street—a bit of a glimmer of pure white against the yellows, reds, and blues. And a red dot that jittered around through the dusty beige curtain almost covering the window. Then he realized what it was.

"Arlene, no! Don't -!"

Without thinking, Gus dove forward and tackled Arlene to the ground. One section of the window burst open, and the bullet from across the street hit the now displaced flat screen TV, knocking it from its homemade bracket on the wall and down to the floor.

Everyone in the hallway hit the floor. The officers in the hall started shouting orders.

"Aw fuck!" Ray exclaimed as he dropped to the ground, well after the fact.

Gus checked Arlene over. She was shaking but unharmed. The gun was out of her hand and had slid underneath an overturned coffee table. He raised his arms slowly and held his hands in an 'O.' He held it there for a moment, then eased himself up to give an all-clear sign. He saw the shadow on the roof across the street recede - the police shooter having left his placement.

Justin went to comfort his stepmom and gave Ray a disgusted look. Ray lost everything he thought he could preserve before a shot was ever fired. The officers moved in, took the cuffed Ray into custody, put a blanket around Justin, and three escorted Arlene out with minimal resistance. The whole ordeal finished just before 8:00 am.

Chapter 2

Despite the fact of it's 'laid back' image, Los Angeles is a highly active city. People are up and moving in the early hours and committing to all sorts of tasks and all kinds of daily chores. On this day, some were up for work while a small percentage were awake to work in a more criminal sense. Many were attacking the day because sleep felt like a waste of the time they had to be on this plane.

Dr. Winston Jones was up and facing the calm waters of Toluca Lake just before 9:00 am. With the sun shining on his face, the so-named lake was serenely stretched out before him as he stared into the nothingness where memories and daydreams lay.

The fountain in the middle provided a rhythmic, noisy bath for passing birds. Despite the promise of swans posted on signs all around, it was primarily ducks and the errant seagull that graced the water with their presence.

Dr. Jones was a tall, bald man who soaked the morning sun through his cinnamon brown skin. Lost in his thoughts, he'd stared long in the direction of the water's surface with a flat expression until a nearby quack unsettled and rescued him from a dark memory.

Dr. Jones looked over to the woman sitting at the other end of the bench the two occupied.

She was a warm, somewhat stiff professional-looking white woman with her own thousand-yard stare. Her name tag flatly said Cathy O'Brien. She wiped beads of sweat from her forehead with a personal handkerchief and silently accepted the dryness in her mouth. Just feeding the ducks seemed to be tiring her out. She tossed some breadcrumbs out and watched the ducks gather closer to gulp them down. When she noticed Jones looking her way, she briefly but warmly smiled in his direction.

He returned her friendly energy with a smile of his own, but no words were exchanged between them. A beautiful day was before them, and each fully experiencing its uniqueness was enough.

It was a quiet morning in this highly upscale enclave. Definitely a far cry from the noisy, chaotic panic just a few miles up the road. This was another world and definitively more peaceful. No shabby apartment complexes to host unsavory families with decades of bad history weighing the roofs down. Every multi-level building here was home to one person or family, and every business was a private, seclusive industry.

Even the nearby local bank seemed to echo a withdrawn, posh demeanor. The Vista National Bank branch was designed with classic architecture. It was a physical embodiment of an outlook and worldview that, in many ways, harkened back to the olden times of the 'horse and buggy' when everyone wore fine suits, even if they were just going out to buy milk. This Vista National branch was an older building of character, acknowledging its need for a fair degree of modernization. Four workers in light blue jumpsuits were heeding the call. The three men and one woman were all working around the exterior and agreed upon areas within the interior. Collectively, each of the four made special efforts to stay well out of the way of bank customers so the slow transition from yester-year would not impede the fast pace required for today's financial business.

The branch had all the modern amenities. Exterior-facing ATMs in both the front and back, a seven-position teller counter on one side with a small but secure safety deposit box vault behind that, and, of course, wi-fi, among other things - but the dressings themselves were clearly antique.

Across from the teller counter on the other side of the central lobby, Angela Gutierrez stood smiling behind her cubicle's desk in the personal banking area. She'd worked her way up to the number two person in the branch hierarchy, which wasn't bad at all. She had an easy but distinguished job handling the financial affairs of some of the bank's larger balance clientele and handling things the tellers weren't trained or equipped to do for the general public. Her eyes caught the four workers in the blue jumpsuits out of her periphery as they moved from one place to another. They were still busily working, but on exactly what she didn't know. Those decisions took place between the branch manager and the higher-ups. Be that as it may, for some reason, today, she was more grateful than normal to be in service to others here, at her desk rather than getting her hands dirty.

Seeing the teller line moving so early, she realized it was time for her to get to work busying herself too. She left her workstation area, passed the line for the tellers at the bank lobby's center, and went to the waiting space for seated personal bank customers. It was there she greeted her first customer of the day.

Thankfully, he was one of her favorites. The ever-cheerful Patrick Henry, a debonair black man who'd never accepted full retirement even into his late 70s. With his fashion sense seemingly stuck in a bygone era, he, understandably, looked as if he'd walked straight out of an 80s supper club in his bright blue suit and crisply polished leather shoes. The suit was something he owned and had worn until it faded from one funky blue to another, but the matching checker-patterned fedora covering his head stylishly set the ensemble off 'just so.'

Looking up and to his right upon her arrival, he smiled wide enough that she could see how his personal magic worked back in his day. He was, indeed, a charmer.

"Good morning Mr. Henry," she chimed. "Well... aren't you sharp today? How've you been?"

Mr. Henry doffed his fedora to her and held it over his walker.

"Fine," he began. "Not as fine as you, but I'm still on this side of the grass."

Angela gave him a playful wink. "Don't you start - I'm gonna be a married woman."

He looked elated. "Say what? When you get snapped up?"

"Well, not yet," she admitted. "One of these days, though."

After their shared laugh, she took a moment while Mr. Henry donned his fedora back onto his head with a bit of effort. Once the distraction passed, she couldn't help but inquire... "Need a little help?" She asked.

"Naw, I got it," he insisted.

Spry as he sounded, without the walker, he couldn't make his rounds to the bank or anywhere else for that matter. She knew it, and he knew it, but they were both too kind to say anything about it. She patiently stood by and waited as he got up.

He turned back to a man - Farhad Ahmadi – who was noticeably gaunt with slightly sallow skin. Mr. Ahmadi was thin enough that he seemed to almost disappear into the lobby's background while facing the bank's rear doors, which opened to the parking lot. Around his waist, he wore a fanny pack of all things.

Both he and Mr. Henry casually nodded to one another as an ending to their seated conversation. Angela saw them looking at one another and turned to the man. "Someone will be right with you, sir," she confirmed.

Ahmadi gave her a light nod in return for her courtesy.

"After you," she offered to Mr. Henry.

"Oh, no," he insisted. "After you."

She walked out ahead of him.

The still seated Mr. Ahmadi casually reached for something inside of his satchel as Mr. Henry began walking away, following Angela dutifully.

The two tennis balls on the front legs of the walker made just enough noise for him to mutter a soft, rascally but unheard "Look at gawd," as Angela's hips wiggled her butt as she led the way.

Two uniformed guards were leaving the teller section through the always-locked area door. As they exited this part of the bank, one guard held a plastic-cased money bag from the vault while the other held his hand firmly on his gun, which is standard procedure in case of emergencies. The guards exited the area in tandem and moved smartly toward the rear doors and into the parking lot.

Then, a muffled gunshot. And another.

Even with the silencer, the second shot was the one that scattered the ducks and other birds at their feet. A deep, dark red oozed out of Cathy O'Brien's chest as she slumped backward, dropping her remaining breadcrumbs. After a moment, the ducks flew back and shuffled forward. It was the first time most of those birds had ever heard a sound louder than their own quack in this neighborhood. They again bit at the bread on the ground around her feet as Dr. Jones stood before her. He quickly but calmly holstered his gun, covering it with his jacket and gently closing her eyes with the first two fingers of his left hand.

Casually glancing around and seeing no one else near the lake, he walked away while taking out an old disposable model phone.

It was 9:11 am. Still early for most, but there was work that needed to get done.

He hit the redial button and held it to his ear as he sauntered away from the lake toward the residential street.

"We're in play," he said. "You good? Guards are gone, right?" He listened while walking, nodded, and unconsciously picked up his pace.

"On my way to you guys now. Remember, we need at least two. Out."

He snapped the phone shut and swapped it for a clear bottle from his deep inner pocket filled with tan-colored liquid makeup. He gave it a shake. The color turned a shade brighter as it aerated.

Arriving on the street, he fumbled with a fob to unlock and enter a newer model Volvo with custom tinted windows. It looked like the car was stuck in nighttime from its exterior. He slipped in, adjusted the seat for his height and leg length, and glanced over at the passenger side floor.

There was a mid-sized duffle bag, half-stuffed, that indicated his readiness for the next phase. He sighed a grunt of effort and was about to head off when he glanced at the mirrors and realized seeing required too much physical exertion. A few minor adjustments later, he was ready to go and smoothly pulled away from the curb.

Once on his way, he sat the still-closed make-up bottle in the passenger seat and speed dialed his phone with the speaker on. It rang twice, then 'Sheila' picked up on the other end.

"Yo."

"You guys set?" he asked.

"Just waiting on your go."

"Alright. Maybe ten minutes." It was a quick, efficient call. A quick, efficient operation.

Back at the Vista National parking lot, the four workers remained spread out completing their various tasks. They each kept watch and communicated with one another via hidden mics and earpieces.

The one named George watched via a reflection in the window he was pretending to clean when a green sedan pulled up and around to the drive-up ATM parking spaces. The ones specifically for quick get-in/get-out transactions.

All four of the worker's duties included keeping track of things, people, and situations... all while appearing industrious in service to the bank. So, George, Lisa, Manuel, and Jimmy, were all far busier than they seemed because today was when the real project was finally going to happen.

The driver of the green car, a mother, named Patricia, turned off the ignition, but the engine continued to try and function until it finally sputtered to a stop.

Patricia prepared to step out of her vehicle. She had the door cracked open while she checked for her wallet. Her daughter, Janelle, was in the back and happily playing with her stuffed toys a little purple elephant and a dark-skinned fairy doll with glittery wings.

Expecting only to be gone for such a short time, she wouldn't even need to tell her daughter she'd be back in a second.

Patricia stepped out, walked up to the ATM, and slid in her card -.

Insufficient Funds. $37 Balance.

So, it was not going to be a quick transaction. She clicked her heel in a huff, took her debit card back from the machine, and returned to her car to open the back door and undo Janelle's harness.

"Mommy needs to go inside the bank Pumpkin," she said.

Janelle fussed with her a little bit and tried to move her hands where her mother's hands were.

"I can do it! I can do it!" the girl insisted. She tried on her own, and it was easier for Patricia to allow her to. The small delay felt like a big time-sink as she waited for the toddler to toddle the locks loose. She finally freed herself from the harness belts.

"That's my girl," Patricia said. "Okay, let's go. Put that down, honey."

"No," Janelle insisted. "Sparkle comes too -."

"Baby, we don't have time for -."

"I want my Daddy -!"

"Okay fine," Patricia relented again. She held her hand out for Janelle to attach to, but Janelle hugged Sparkle instead, with both hands.

"Fine. Whatever. Just - let's go."

Janelle climbed down and ran up to take her mother's hand after Patricia retracted it. George walked in front of them and held the door open as they went in. Patricia walked at a pace Janelle could not match. She was trying to get things done quickly - too quick to even nod in his general direction or to offer a curt and passive-aggressive thanks.

Unaffected by her unintentional rudeness, Patricia's desire for expedience wouldn't be fast enough for George. He pulled out a walkie-talkie once the two were inside the bank.

"This is Zebra 4," he quietly announced. "We now have one on the inside. One on the inside and 15 total. Over."

He put the radio down and reached into his tool bag. He took out a set of wireless speakers, black, innocuous, and hid them in the bushes on either side of the bank's rear entrance. He then scanned the perimeter: no one watching, nothing else going on.

It felt like the easy in-and-out job was about to get a touch more involved and a few degrees more complicated.

Because it was.

Chapter 3

H is adrenaline settling down and feeling the warmth of the LA morning sun, Gus stood by and watched the interrogation of his rescued perpetrators. At his request, Arlene was not in cuffs, and Justin was right beside her. The counselors were both fair and sincere in how they were treating her because they had Gus' word; she wasn't a danger. Yes, she had been the one with the gun and the one with the hostage, but she was also the one with the massive black eye and bruises old and new. Justin was hovering protectively, but that, ultimately, wouldn't make much difference.

To amuse himself, Gus tried to trade glances with Captain Logan on the scene, but Logan didn't bite and simply ignored him. Not even a dogged glare in his general direction. Just a cold shoulder and a bite at a donut.

It was all procedure from there. The sensitive work he did to save every life in that building had to be buried under the next few days' worths of paperwork and objective-based reporting. Nothing about the emotional toll it would take, the cost in tears and sweat the family would now have to suffer. Just statements, testimonies, and the crapshoot that she could get out on low bail.

Glancing at his watch, Gus walked away toward Captain Powell, the red-haired lady of iron who commanded the operation.

"Captain -." He said.

"Detective," she immediately interrupted. "Nice work up there. You're getting that mojo back. How's the kid?"

Gus rolled it off and went with her conversation instead.

"Fine. He'll be better off with that 'dip-shit' daddy of his in prison."

"Piece of work, that one," she said with a shake of her head. "What's up?"

"Wondering if I can get outta here? I've got a standing Skype time with my kid, and my ex -" Gus lamented.

"Yeah, yeah," she interrupted again. "Go. What did you do to that poor woman anyway? She stays in your ass."

"Other than breathe?" he shrugged. "Hell, not win the lotto." He could see the captain was not receptive to his assessment. "What can I say? She left me for the guy with big money."

"Ah. Helluva thing," she said. "Well... It gets better. 'Least that's what they say."

She left Gus nodding to himself while she turned and immediately addressed an officer waiting in the wings.

"Stevie Pete? This man just caused you more paperwork."

Officer Peters, first name Steven, tilted his head back with a short-cut sigh. "Oh, for crying out - Yes, ma'am," he bit his tongue and saluted with the sincerity her rank deserved.

"Thank you, Captain," Gus said. He saluted her as well.

She snapped one back and walked off in a military gait. Officer Peters followed her a few measured steps behind.

"You owe me," he muttered. "Big time."

Gus smirked and bit a laugh between his teeth to stifle it.

"Everybody owes you, Stevie Pete. Everybody..." Gus quietly joked.

Peters smirked at him on his way past. That freed Gus to leave as soon as he could get through the police line to his car. He excused himself past the barricades and, out of habit, checked to see if his car had any new bruises. But having gotten rear-ended into another vehicle in stop-and-go traffic on the 134 East a few days prior meant he was wasting his time.

At least he'd done a good job parking in his rush to get to the third-floor commotion earlier.

The driver-side door made a hideous enough sound that a few cops turned to see Gus ignore their stares. Of course, Logan looked over Gus' way and smiled condescendingly.

Now Gus was pissed but had nowhere to direct the anger, which worsened things. He got in and turned the key. The engine was on his side in spirit, but the battery wasn't generating any real power to help. The car sputtered, stuttered, shuddered - and did everything but start. Gus cranked the key again and pumped the pedal. Then the brake, which didn't help. Then he tried working the lights on and off to see if that might somehow light a spark.

"C'mon, not now," he whispered.

Nothing. He sighed his head back into his seat and got out for a light jog back through the police line where nobody laughed - to his face.

"Officer Peters," Gus called out.

"Oh, now I've got a title?" Stevie Pete replied.

He immediately realized the problem since Gus was in front of him, rather than several blocks away.

"When's your insurance gonna fix that thing?"

Gus shook his head.

"They're still deciding whether or not it's totaled. Bastards treat me like I hit-and-ran myself. Jump me?"

Peters sighed with a shrug of his shoulders and weighed the addition of yet another favor onto his back.

"Sure," he said. "Let me pull a car over. Again."

Gus nodded to him, thankfully. He checked his watch. Time was running short. It was already 9:22.

9:22. Dr. Jones was almost ready. His practiced five-minute make-up job took just under four. He went from being early 50s with smooth, still youthful brown skin to having a few noticeable wrinkles and looking white. The mask was a firm silicone with some flexibility, not the type to flap around, and was tight all over his head. He fitted his wig on next, short, conservative-looking, silvery locks. Fake up close but decently real at a distance.

He checked himself in the overhead mirror. Even his eyelids were white. Gray-ish on a close inspection, but nothing out of the ordinary for such a pedestrian-looking man. Otherwise, everything looked fine.

His cell phone rang, and he put it on speaker. 'George' was calling. "We have one inside and have maybe 20 or so all together," he reported.

"Good," Jones replied. "No more burner phones. Melt 'em and switch to walkies. Pass the word."

He hung up and threw the phone into the duffle bag and all his used makeup tools into the plastic bag next to him. Then he pulled off, mere minutes from the rendezvous for his little chore at Vista National Bank.

Meanwhile, the bank stayed busy with morning activity. Patricia waited impatiently in the lobby for a teller to open up. Her eyes went from generic morning news on the TVs in the lobby to her watch and only just glancing in her daughter's direction.

She saw a dark, sparkly object fly just past her legs and onto the floor. Little Sparkle took a tumble, and Janelle looked proud of it.

"Janelle?" Patricia said in a loud hush. Her daughter wasn't listening. "Janelle!" she added a bit of anger to her whisper. "Pick her up, honey." Janelle looked back at her. Like she didn't understand why Sparkle had to be there. "Now! 1, 2 -," Janelle responded to the counting with a pout. "Do you want a time out when we get home? Janelle -?"

"No!" Janelle insisted. "No time out. Mommy. No time out!"

Patricia looked up. A teller was just freed up at the window second closest to the rear doors and waved for Patricia to come over.

Patricia reflexively scanned the room and saw a small corner of the lobby with some distracting toys and blocks on a little table near the front doors. "Honey," she said, "you and Sparkle can play over there."

Janelle immediately grabbed Sparkle like it was no big deal and ran off to play.

Patricia sighed and walked up to the window, to Carmelita, who was watching patiently from behind the glass.

"Good morning, and welcome to Vista," they said. "How can I help you today?"

"Um, I have a situation," she began, in a tone that told Carmelita that everything she was about to say was absolutely correct. "I was told by another teller—who I don't see here right now, of course – that a check I deposited four days ago would be available today, and I just came from the ATM and –"

"I understand," Carmelita said. "Okay, slide your card, please."

They motioned to the reader on the side and leaned in a little to the glass while Patricia followed through.

"Your little girl is an absolute DOLL!" they said with hushed excitement.

Patricia graciously accepted the compliment and smiled while she scanned her card.

Janelle, in the meantime, was ready to play when she noticed her company, the very thin Middle Eastern man from earlier, Mr. Ahmadi, who was still waiting with his hands folded over his lap. They exchanged a quiet pleasantry of smiles with one another.

"Hi," she greeted.

He greeted her back with tired but smiling eyes and a whisper of a voice that sounded much older than he appeared to be.

"Hello, little one. You – you are a blessing to me."

"Hi," she repeated.

She held up the fairy. "This is Sparkle. My mommy bought-ed her." She showed the fairy off and made it wave to him.

"Beautiful," he said. "Hello, Sparkle."

Janelle went on to play in the toy corner while he watched over her from his seat. Patricia could only see her daughter from where she stood at the teller counter and was glad to see her quietly distracted by the clacking toys.

"She's a handful," she admitted, "but thank you."

Carmelita studied the computer screen with a slightly increasing concern. "Um, I guess it's because of the dollar amount? When –"

"I deposited it four days ago," Patricia explained. "The other teller said it would take three business days to clear and –"

"I think there's a 7-day hold on -."

"-No!" Patricia insisted. "That's not what she told me. I've got checks that -."

"Hold on, hold on," Carmelita insisted. "I'm just telling you what the bank's policies are."

Patricia gave a firm, silent nod. She'd heard that line before and was waiting for better news.

"I'll bet I know who told you it would be three days, but we not gonna go there right now. Okay?" Carmelita leaned forward and offered a quiet, helpful, conspiratorial tone. "Let me see what I can do. Give me a sec?"

Patricia nodded more sincerely, thoughtfully.

Carmelita walked to an office door behind the teller glass and near the front of the bank. It was the office door of Cathy O'Brien, the branch manager.

But the office was empty.

Seeing that, Carmelita turned to the nearest employee, Ronald, the handsome young son of southeast Asian immigrants.

"Ronald... question. Any idea when Cathy's due in? I've got a large check issue –"

"Hey, look," Ronald responded, with a sudden upturn of tone, "I don't know where Cathy is. You might want to, um, check with Angela. She's the boss when Cathy's not—Hold up."

Ronald spotted Angela across the lobby and stood up to wave to get her attention. She was still in the middle of speaking with her client, Mr. Henry, whose back was facing the lobby area. He, without question, wasn't about to start moving again until his matter was settled.

Angela then noticed Ronald signaling he wanted to place a call to her desk as he picked his phone up.

"—for both of your grand kids? Yes. And by connecting them to your account, we can avoid inheritance tax issues as long as the money is transferred in before, uh –."

She paused for a moment to find a better way to say what needed to be said.

"Before I head off to the Big Dance in the sky?" he filled in.

She smiled and nodded quickly. "Yes. Before you – go to the dance."

Her phone rang as Ronald dialed over to her.

"Sorry, I need to grab this."

Mr. Henry nodded and let her take up the call. While she did, he reached into the breast pocket of his shirt and took out two pills. No bottle, no blister pack, no packaging. Just two loose pills that he held between well-worn fingers that were barely strong enough to clutch them. He stared at them for a moment, inhaled a long, thoughtful breath of air and exhaled while he absorbed the purpose they would serve before, finally, slipping them back in. He shook off the weight of his thoughts with a sip of water and waited for his banker to do whatever it was that caused the call.

"This is Angela." She began her service with Ronald across the lobby. Ronald worked on his computer as he explained and then processed the request for Carmelita.

Carmelita watched over Ronald's shoulder and paid particular attention to the body connected to his shoulder while waiting for what they hoped would be good news.

Meanwhile, Patricia kept a watchful eye on the tellers working on her request, noting that the issue seemed more complicated than she'd anticipated. She also kept watching her busy little daughter.

Janelle, of course, continued to play in the toy corner when she suddenly became captivated by a puzzle box configuration that was also there.

It was this toy that caused her to put Sparkle down.

At the same time, Janelle discovered the puzzle box; in strode through the front doors, an extraordinarily tall man, not quite seven feet tall but close enough, with hair as grey as storm clouds that was slicked back in thick wisps.

Understandably, more than a few customers noticed him.

He entered with a COVID mask over the lower part of his face and avoided the other seats in the lobby waiting area nearest Janelle and sat down directly next to Mr. Ahmadi.

The two men shared a slight but rather severe nod with one another as he sat.

A few more customers entered through each set of doors, their current business, other errands, and individual tasks on their minds.

It was a bank. People were banking and doing what they did. Several people had specific, unspoken deeds yet to complete.

All of this just after 9:40 am.

Chapter 4

G us got his car going a few minutes after he thought he would be leaving, but indeed, he still had plenty of time to see and speak with his son on their scheduled call.

He pulled over on the side of the road not even a block away from the still active police scene with his phone up and burning through roaming data on a video call with Tricia, a teenager who was out of her depth in dealing with his growing agitation.

"But," he began, pausing to cool his head. "How is he taking a nap when the call was supposed to start not even 10 minutes ago? He can't be asleep already!"

Tricia looked away from the screen to respond to someone standing just off-screen. The person who he was really dealing with.

"Uh... Sorry you missed him Mr. Martin. But I've got to hang up now. Take care."

Without further warning, the screen suddenly went dark, the new equivalent of the clap of a phone slamming into its receiver. Gus took a deep breath and shuddered it out, then repeated as he dialed until his breath came out as smooth as the rush of air from passing cars. Just a regular call this time, so he wouldn't be heard in his harried state by a law firm employee.

"Yes," Gus opened the call. "Theodore Gold, please. Augustus Martin.... Yes, I'm a client – Look, I don't care. Tell him it is an emergency!"

He sighed as he let the anger overcome him for a moment, but it worked. A moment later, he was connected to Theo Gold of Stevenson, Gold & Drew Law Offices.

"Mr. Martin," Theo answered, with his voice always at a slight tinge of arrogance. "Good...morning," he had to check what time it was. "I'm about to head to Court shortly. What's up?"

"What's up? What's up?!" Gus repeated with ascending frustration. "Theo, this - I won't use that word - won't let me see or talk to my kid! There's gotta be something you can do. Can't you file some type of order the judge will listen to?"

"Mr. Martin... I want to do the right thing here. Really." He didn't sound sincere. "But you've got an outstanding bill that's grown quite large –."

"My God!" Gus gasped. "You've billed me over $85,000 in less than two years! I've given you everything—Hell, you told me you thought it would take $15,000 when all this bullshit started!"

"But you owe almost 3/4ths of that, sir, and I also told you that figure was an estimate... an average –"

"And," Gus interrupted, "it's costing me five times that because she doesn't follow the orders and hasn't suffered one repercussion. Not one!"

Theo sighed, a temporary break in his composure of knowing everything. "Mr. Martin... we worked very hard to get you an extremely favorable visitation schedule –"

"Which she has yet to follow!" Gus exclaimed. "I haven't seen my kid in-person for almost four months now! Now this... 'person' won't even allow Skype calls unless she feels like it."

Another sigh, back to business. "Can you raise or borrow a reasonable deposit for –"

"From where?" Gus asked. "I've given you everything I have. Hell, I paid you thirty grand from a Home Equity Line of Credit on a house I don't even have anymore! The fuck –"

"Your ex-wife," Theo replied with an equal rise in tone, "is using the income disparity between the two of you to make a mockery of the Judge's Orders for your case. Unfortunately, it takes money to fight money in these –"

"I know!" Gus exclaimed back. He drew his tone back down as much as he could, but there was no helping it in his case. "I just want to see my kid Mr. Gold. I just want to see my kid!"

There was a brief pause as Theo seemingly nodded to share the concern.

"I don't mean to be condescending Mr. Martin… but I am running a business. I have people that work for me, and I have to be able to –"

"—you have to be able to pay them. I know. Shit… I know."

"As soon as you can make a reasonable dent in the—in your bill. You have my word. Your case will be my priority. And… again, another option you have is that you can sign a Change of Attorney form -"

"So, I can represent myself," he finished. "Yeah. I think we both know how that goes. Okay. I understand."

"Have a good day, Mr. Martin," Theo said.

Gus hung up first and sat back in his seat. All the rage in his face turned into moisture in his eyes. He was left nowhere better than when he started and still couldn't see his kid in any form except the picture on his pendant. Just three-and-a-half years old. At this rate, which was the purpose, Gus feared his son might forget which of his 'dads' was really his father. He'd had a long night and a rough morning on the job, and now, this shit again… and it was only just 9:52.

…

9:52. She intentionally hadn't looked at her watch in what had felt like hours but had only been about 30 minutes. These department-by-department 'dog and pony show' meetings were supposedly for her benefit to bring her up to speed, but Commissioner Evelyn Kennedy had studied the LAPD policy and procedure manuals as well as upper management emails that sent orders that flew in the face of those procedural directives. She knew what went on and what was supposed to be happening, but these meetings were valuable in helping her get to know the team she'd become the Commander for.

While the department heads droned on about objectives, goals and policy Lynn Kennedy was watching behavior... and noting consistency issues. These departmental overviews were perfect platforms to help her determine those attempting to provide what they believed to be valuable information to the new Commissioner and also allowed her to take note of who was seemingly not happy that she was the new Commissioner – for whatever reason.

• • • •

9:57 AM. DR. JONES sat in the last row of the back parking lot with his car facing away from the rear of the bank. He made sure his gloves fit tight and his makeup settled. At a glance, he looked like he had walked out of an old Polish retirement home. He reached for the walkie in his cupholder. "How many? Over."

"Still just the one," the worker named Lisa replied. "Over."

"We can't wait," he replied. "Get ready."

He put the walkie down and picked up his cell phone—one last call. He dialed and the call connected before the first ring ended.

"You've got 10 minutes max. Hit it!" Jones commanded.

He hung up and snapped the phone in half over the emergency brake in the middle console. He then discarded the remains in the plastic trash bag. Jones checked his mirrors in rapid succession and then turned around and pulled a sawed-off shotgun from the duffle bag on the passenger-side floor. Finally, he took out the Glock he'd used at the lake earlier and removed the still-attached silencer because this time, he wanted the noise.

The job was on.

Sheila got the message and exhaled. She was at the other end of Jones' last phone call. She'd gotten the word needed to start her end of things - or continue, as she'd already started and been in a holding pattern, waiting to reach the finish line. She looked back at her victim. The poor man never knew what was coming. She removed the dart lodged in his neck and looked over the duct tape covering his mouth, wrists and ankles, which were bound with zip ties. She stepped out of the driver's seat and met eyes with Bird, her accomplice, among other things. Both had plenty to live for, just in their 30s, black and well-trusted by the good doctor.

They'd donned sunglasses and elastic face masks to keep their faces hidden. They were out of the cars and up to the back door of a remote video security operations center. Right where the electronic eyes for several Vista National Bank branches were located. They pulled out a pair of handguns and knocked rhythmically on the door. The coded knock got the door opened by a nerdy guy with 'Roberts' on the I.D. badge clipped to his belt. He was looking at his watch instead of in their direction for a second too long.

"You're late," he chastised, "and it's - whoa!"

Once he noticed, he was already held up. Sheila shushed him with a finger and quickly moved in with Bird right on her heels.

"Turn around," she said quietly. "Keep calm. Walk back to the control center. Easy."

Roberts nodded and walked through the building as an involuntary, unwitting guide. It was an odd thing – dumb, actually – but she couldn't help wondering why the place that maintained video security didn't have video security.

Her inner questioning stopped once they stood before the control center door, which was locked shut with a keycode on a pad beside the handle.

"Don't make this hard," Sheila whispered. "Your code, NOT the police alert. Got me?"

Roberts nodded and punched in the proper code. The door clicked and then unlocked. Sheila pushed him to the back wall, and Bird took point.

They nodded, guns up. Once the door was opened, Bird stormed in. Two other employees saw him come in and froze in shock.

"Don't touch another button!" Bird demanded. "Stand up. Move back two steps from your consoles. Follow instructions, and you will not be hurt."

The men looked at one another. They saw Roberts in the doorway with a gun to his head.

"Try to be a hero?" Bird was being rhetorical. He cocked his gun. Enough said. The men followed instructions as Sheila moved in.

"Cell phones, thumb drives – everything," she said. "Out of your pockets and on the desks." Orders were followed quickly and quietly. "You two, over there. Now!"

The coworkers ducked their heads and shuffled to the wall with their hands pressed against it.

"You," Bird commanded Roberts with his gun. "Sit. There."

He pointed to the chair in front of the main control panel.

"Cut the feeds to the Glendale, Toluca Lake, and Van Nuys branches."

"But," Roberts said, "that's gonna alert -."

"I know," Bird said impatiently. "And you're gonna take the phone calls. Tell 'em that 'it's nothing major, but the outage should be fixed within 15 minutes.' Don't get cute. Go."

Roberts nodded his head and typed in some commands on the keyboard. In just a few moments, a few of the screens went dark. Roberts put his hands up, no funny business, as long as Bird had him at gunpoint. The seconds dragged by like nails across the LCD displays. Then finally, the phone rang. Three lines rang through pretty much at once.

"Stick to the script, and you're golden," Bird warned. "What's your Employee ID number?"

"What?" Roberts said. He craned his head down to his badge. "471425."

Bird moved the gun up from center mass to his forehead.

Roberts' lip quivered. "280143. I'm sorry," he said.

"Answer."

Roberts took a calming breath and answered in a quick, subdued, and well-rehearsed manner for each one.

"Video Security. Yes, we are aware of the problem. It should be resolved within 15 minutes. Mine? Roberts. Employee ID 280143. Have a good one."

After the third call, he looked over to Bird for approval. He took the butt of the gun to the face and was rocked back a few inches in the rolling chair.

"I told you not to fuck with me! Now get up." Bird handled Roberts to his staggering feet and threw him into the corner.

Sheila checked her watch.

"In exactly four minutes," she explained, "you're gonna turn those two back on."

She motioned to two of the monitors. But not the one for the Toluca Lake branch.

Chapter 5

"Sorry about that," Angela apologized. Mr. Henry nodded politely as she returned her full attention to him. "Branch Manager isn't in yet, and I'm next in the food chain. Where were we now?"

"Attaching accounts, you said," he reminded her. "For my grandchildren?"

"Right!" she nodded. "Okay... I need to grab a couple of forms for you to sign."

She got up and walked to the cubicle area next door. Mr. Henry leaned back when she passed him and gave her rear a lascivious look. While his eyes focused on her, there were no active camera eyes on him or anybody else in or around the bank.

Jones got his walkie for the last time as he grabbed the now full duffle bag and finished strapping up in his car seat.

"Okay. Cut the outgoing wires for the cameras. Now."

Two blue jumpsuit workers, Miguel and Jimmy, got the signal and were in the electronics closet. They pulled two plugs out and plugged two new ones that they'd wired themselves. Every wire to every screen, server, and monitor was under their control.

There might have been a hiccup in the signals sent to the new monitors that had been installed inside, but no one was available to notice. Besides, almost all eyes suddenly fell onto the very tall, older gentleman as he rose and strode toward the men's restroom. Miguel and Jimmy walked through the main lobby in-route to their next positions while Carmelita and Patricia finished up their legitimate business at the counter.

"So," Carmelita began, "we were able to release twenty-five hundred dollars because of the little mix-up, and the remainder will be released in two more days. And your cash," they handed it out under the glass slot, "fifty, 2, fifty, 3, fifty, four hundred."

Patricia counted along with a satisfied grin.

"Thank you so much." She stacked the bills and arranged them into her purse. "Today started like a nightmare. Thank you!"

"Have a great rest of your day," they said.

Patricia left the window, walked over to the little toy area, and noticed the thin stranger sitting nearby. She gave him a stiff, courteous smile, and he nodded back with a slow, tired blink as he wiped the sweat from his brow.

"Come on, baby," Patricia insisted. "Time to go."

Her daughter wasn't listening. She was nearly halfway through her puzzle cube.

"Janelle -."

"Can I play five more minutes?" she asked, sounding disappointed.

"Baby," Patricia began, "We've got another couple of stops, and then MAYBE we can get to the park before nap time, okay?"

"Yay!" Janelle exclaimed. She jumped up from the puzzle box. "We're going to the park! We're going to the park!" She started jumping around in place.

"I said maybe – Oh Lord."

Patricia grabbed Janelle's hand and tried to power walk an enthusiastic Janelle to the rear exit where they'd come in.

The last of the four blue jump-suited workers picked up a walkie and huddled into the corner to announce, "She's about to leave!"

Patricia almost got all the way to the bank's rear doors when Janelle stopped her fast.

"Mommy, where's Sparkle?"

"See?" Patricia whispered in an admonishing tone. "That's why I told you to leave her in the car."

She saw her tone had Janelle somewhere between upset and sad. She tried to help shake the miscue off for her daughter.

"I'm sorry, baby. I've just got a lot on my mind. But that's no excuse. I should never be mean. You be a big girl and go get Sparkle –"

"All by myself!" Janelle said happily. She skipped back across to the play area while Patricia checked her watch and then turned to gaze at a television screen on the lobby wall.

Dr. Jones looked up from his watch with a deep breath through his rubber lips. He put sunglasses on over his fake ears and cracked open the door. His walkie screeched at him. "We caught a break," Jimmy said. "On your count."

Jones picked up the walkie and held the button down.

"In 5, 4, 3 - WAIT!"

He watched in the side mirror as a car slowed right down on the side road behind him and to his left, its signal flickering as the driver turned in. The car rolled past directly behind him, parked, and a large man stepped out of the vehicle enough to rock it while letting his two kids out of the back, a little girl and a bratty older boy.

George saw them all coming and laid his ladder flat in the foliage. He went to the door and held it open for them, then followed them all inside. No one else was on the side street. Nobody coming or going. They were clear. Jones stepped out, fully strapped and disguised.

"Okay. 5, 4, 3 -" Jones counted down into the walkie.

10:13. Jimmy knocked at the teller's door. Carmelita opened it, let him in, and pointed him back to the employee break room. He was sweating profusely, looked a bit ill, and walked behind everyone on the teller's side. He turned his back to the tellers and unzipped his jumpsuit to reach for what was inside.

The newly arrived father got in the teller line and pointed his kids to the play area where Janelle was recovering Sparkle. Patricia was still watching the news on the monitors on the back wall, skimming the headlines and tickers along the bottom. The two new kids waved at Janelle but maintained social distancing as they'd all been taught.

Lisa walked over to the personal banking area and headed straight for the open-air cubicles where Angela and Mr. Henry were engaged in filling-out long forms. Lisa stood by for a moment until she saw someone outside marching steadily toward the rear entrance. She unzipped her suit and reached down for her gun.

Jones entered calmly through the doors, an older man with a rifle. He aimed at the ceiling and shot out a few tiles with a burst of rounds.

"On the floor," he demanded. He tossed the duffel bag onto the floor at his feet. "Do not look at me. Do not look at me! Lay on the floor and close your eyes! Do it now!"

Panic had begun, and one of the kids started to scream. Patricia immediately started running toward the toy area of the lobby.

Jones repeated: "Get on the floor!" with fierce urgency.

He pulled out his handgun and aimed it across the way. Everyone dove for the floor or lowered themselves as fast as their wide, old bodies would let them. The tellers behind the desk were in a panic, except for Ronald. He reached for the panic button but felt something stiff and angular at the back of his head. He heard a hushing sound from the man, quietly insisting that he not push that button.

Patricia was the only one still moving. She made a dive into the play area to Janelle as Jones shot twice.

There was a tense, awful silence.

Patricia first landed on the ground with a sliding thud before slowly opening her eyes. She felt nothing. She looked down at Janelle in her arms. No blood. No gunshot. She looked around at the rest of the area. Her eyes crossed something that made her body shiver.

"Mommy!" Janelle screamed.

"Everything's okay, baby," she whispered reassuringly. "We have to stay here and do what the man says."

She held Janelle tight to her chest and kept her head low so Janelle wouldn't see the blood oozing out of the now slumping Middle Eastern man's chest. Other customers also saw the late Mr. Ahmadi, and their silence begat their future cooperation.

"Listen!" Jones declared again. "Cooperate, and you will not be harmed. Fail to cooperate, and you'll get what he got. This is a robbery, but not of your money. One at a time, we will allow you to complete your bank transactions. Keep your eyes closed until you are blindfolded. Follow instructions."

He picked up the duffel bag and walked toward the center of the bank, with everyone in sight.

"As long as there are no heroes, everything will go smoothly! In a few seconds, you will take out your cell phones and lay them next to you. I want ALL cell phones, any weapons and/or self-defense gadgets you have. Today is NOT the day to be brave. I won't warn you again. Do it!"

Almost everyone complied as he spoke, but a few waited for his final command to start. He saw phones come out, mace, whistles, chains, and even one handgun.

The tellers behind the glass did the same, with Miguel and Jimmy holding them to the doctor's word. Only one person wasn't complying and didn't look like they planned on doing so.

"Hey!" Jones called out. He turned fully to Mr. Henry. "Why are YOU not on the floor?"

"60 seconds!" Jimmy called out.

Mr. Henry stared at Dr. Jones' fake eyelids across the lobby with an unshakeable, calm fury. "You go to hell, you son of a bitch! You should be ashamed of yourself!"

"Suit yourself, old man," Jones said. He calmly aimed at the defiant senior with the handgun.

Angela stood up on her knees with her eyes firmly shut and waved her hands in Jones' vague direction.

"No, wait!" she shouted. "WAIT! Please don't shoot! He'll cooperate. We all will." She reached over to Mr. Henry, but he shrugged her off.

"Do it," he insisted. "Shoot. I'm not afraid of you. If today's my day, then so be it!"

"NO!" Angela shouted. "Mr. Henry! Just face me, okay? Face me. Don't look at them."

After an angry hesitation, Mr. Henry turned the back of his chair to Jones with a curmudgeonly groan, for her sake. Jones lowered his gun slowly. Angela felt around to ensure Mr. Henry was turned her way and sat on the floor next to him, her back to the center of the bank.

Jones walked over to them and waved for Lisa to come over.

"Okay, miss. Get up," he commanded. "Finish up with this old motherfucker and then anything the other customers want done."

Angela nodded compliantly and got up to sit behind her desk.

Once Lisa arrived, Jones ensured everyone in the immediate area could hear. "You watch. Kill the first hero, you see." She nodded and put her eyes on the people in the personal banking area.

Jones turned to address the rest of the bank interior.

"You'll be blindfolded and separated. Bank employees with bank employees and customers over here. Old man? Let's see if you make it to the end of the day."

Mr. Henry remained defiant, now ignoring Jones with passively aggressive stiffened shoulders. Jones walked across to where the three children were lying down on the ground, along with Patricia, the mother, who had almost taken bullets to her back.

"I can see that you two are courageous. Who are you here with?"

The boy said nothing but stood up and put himself between Dr. Jones and his sister protectively. His sister then spoke up. "My daddy!" she exclaimed.

"Three minutes!" Jimmy called out.

"Good," Jones said. "Point him out to me, please."

She got up and walked over to the big man on the floor where the teller line had been. The one guy who'd pulled out a revolver of all things when asked to empty his pockets.

"My daddy is strong, and he can beat you up!" she declared.

Jones looked down at the man. He could see that he wasn't just a wide load; he also had solid thickness in his arms.

"I believe you... but I really hope he doesn't try to beat me up. Go into that office back there, sweetheart." he said, pointing behind the glass to the manager's office.

He waved to the still-standing boy, Chris, who worked hard to appear unafraid while looking down at the floor.

"Young man? Please go and take care of your sister and," he now pointed to Janelle, "you, young lady. Take your doll and go with them. Now, please."

Patricia let go of Janelle and looked her in the eyes.

"Go on, baby," she said quietly. "Mommy's fine."

Janelle clutched Sparkle tight and began walking. Chris walked to shield her from seeing the old, dead man in the chair. The kids were ushered through the teller-side door and were walked into the office.

Once gone and without warning, Jones heel kicked the father of two in his side, silently daring him to get up. The man groaned but did not budge.

"Okay. You will all now get up but continue looking downward. Not at us. You employees go on that side of the glass. If I find anything on you – anything—you will wind up like this gentleman."

He again pointed over to the dead Mr. Ahmadi in the chair.

"Move!"

The shuffle began. Miguel herded the tellers and other bankers, aside from Angela, to the teller side of the glass. Lisa, meanwhile, continued to hold the peace on the Personal Banking side.

"Hands behind your back!" she demanded.

Jones fired another burst from his rifle into the ceiling to speed things along.

"We will have company very soon..." he said to himself.

It was all going exactly to plan inside the building. From outside, anyone a block away or more likely wouldn't hear anything or would pass it off as they continued along with their day. Vista National wasn't the bank of choice for Toluca Lake, but it was sizeable enough to get the job done. However, just like Mr. Henry and Patricia and all the rest, it did still have its regulars.

And one was outside the rear doors, looking in from a relatively safe distance. She saw the muzzle flashes and heard the shots, watched a man walk around authoritatively in the middle and all the employees get cordoned off to one side - she knew what was happening and fearfully retreated to call 911.

Chapter 6

F irst, the call went to the dispatchers working out of the greater LA area and surrounding counties. The dispatcher took the call from the woman at the scene.

"Thank you for holding 911. Wait – Who is shooting, ma'am? From inside the bank or—Could you see – Okay, are you in a safe location? No. Ma'am, I need you to leave your vehicle where it is and move away from the bank until we have officers in place. Please protect yourself and stay on the line."

Then the dispatcher found officers near the crime scene to send to hold ground before alerting a supervisor.

"Phil! We've got a bank robbery. Over in Toluca Lake - Vista National. Reports of gunfire, suspects are armed and dangerous."

Given the severity of the report, the dispatcher also transferred to a general line for all units in the area.

"Calling all units, be advised, shots fired, shots fired. We have a two-eleven in progress at Vista National, Riverside Drive and Forman Avenue. One suspect is a tall White male, gray hair –" and the report continued to follow the caller's account.

Officers in the area responded as necessary. The responding officers would confirm their positions and arrivals and work up the chain to the on-station department heads for further instruction while maintaining regular safety protocols as their training dictated.

For a bank robbery, with live gunfire, pulled off without any silent alarms or security center provisional calls, the situation was deemed critical and something far more than just a simple in-and-out quick job. It required the efficacy and organization of the higher-level officials with the force. The one most obviously available close to the time of the robbery and on active duty at City Hall was, of course, Commissioner Kennedy.

Michelle, a new, overwhelmed, and overrun assistant, practically ran in during the conference with various department heads and slowed to make a sorry, shuffling march toward Lynn.

"Ma'am?" she uttered in the most polite, subservient whisper she could. "Um, I'm sorry to disturb –."

"It's okay," Lynn said, also whispering. "What is it?"

"The —," she began nervously, "your secretary said to tell you that there's a bank robbery that..."

"That what?"

"They think there are hostages, ma'am—I mean, Commissioner. At risk."

Lynn nodded and processed the information calmly.

"Okay. Focus. Where is Randall?"

"Randall?"

"Yes, Jeff Randall," she said. "My assistant. Find him, tell him about this and have him keep me informed of the situation. Got it?"

"Um, yes," she responded.

Quickly and apologetically, she walked back out. Commissioner Kennedy refocused on the meeting and reflexively reached for her wrist for self-comfort. Her fingers brushed against her wedding ring on the way. She glanced at it quickly and subconsciously decided to slowly twist it around and around on her finger.

It wasn't quite 11 am yet, and crime around the city was both unusual and at full throttle....

• • • •

GUS WAS ESPECIALLY tired; there was hardly time to settle in after the emergency call to work last night. He'd reached his apartment and barely had the energy to register his arrival. His desk and kitchen were in a clear state of 'hot mess.' He had far too much furniture in the now, much smaller living space. Even though it was all high quality by 'regular folk' standards, he kept wanting to sell some of it off for a fresh start, but there wasn't anything that he wanted to part with. Not really.

He chugged down the last of the coffee he didn't recall buying, lukewarm at best, collapsed on the couch, and shielded his eyes from the sun while lying against the armrest to get some much-needed shut-eye.

As Gus drifted off, the rest of the city moved with ever-increasing speed. Vista National Bank was surrounded in a matter of minutes. The woman who'd made the 911 call was escorted away from the street corner she'd retreated to. Lights were blaring, but no sirens. Two cops jumped from their vehicles, shielded themselves with car doors, and held position with guns aimed at the bank's back doors. Captain Logan showed up with a bullet proof vest already on at the farther end of the parking lot. He ran communications with the other squad cars in the fleet.

"Officer Peters. Report."

Stevie Pete was in the front of the bank, holding position with his car door as protective armor. He checked behind him. The street was already blocked off. Two more cars flanked him, creating a sort of roofless door-to-door bunker. Everyone had vests on and weapons out. He picked up the radio and replied.

"Peters here. Traffic is diverted, and the front of the bank is secured. I can see movement inside but cannot, repeat, cannot determine the number of people involved. Over."

Captain Logan heard the report and opened to an all-channel broadcast.

"All Officers, listen up. Maintain your positions but do not advance. Repeat... do not advance at this time. Nobody goes in or out of the perimeter unless I say so. Stay on your toes. Dispatch? Go ahead and make the call. I'm ready."

Within seconds, the telephone on Ronald's desk began ringing. Angela's phone too. Every other line was already cut. Jimmy had seen to that. Now he was on the hustle after getting a hand signal and a verbal request from Jones.

"Toss me the mic," he said.

Jimmy reached into his satchel and pulled out a wireless microphone. He underhanded it over the glass screen, and Jones caught it in a solid grip. He clicked on the microphone. Wireless speakers placed all around the bank activated outside. Jones waited for the phones to stop ringing, so his digitally altered voice came through clear - and a whole decibel range lower.

"Infidels! We do not negotiate. Comply with our demands, or lives will be lost, and all blood will be on your hands. First, write down one cell phone number as your point of contact. We contact you—you do not contact us. Period. If you cut our electricity, someone will die. If you cut our air conditioning or water, someone dies. We have your precious money and many lives at our disposal, including children. All police will now retreat to a minimum distance of 20 meters. You have 30 seconds to comply."

He turned the mic off, pocketed it, and then pointed to the dead man. "Take off his fanny pack and then go grab one of the kids!"

"Please," the big man who'd given up the gun said. "No!"

Jones looked down with ire at his upstart hostage.

Outside, Captain Logan and the rest of the force interpreted the threat and counted the seconds from when the warning ended. Logan picked up his radio and conducted the group.

"Hold your current position. We will not bow down to terrorists. Peters? Get me into the bank video feed to get an idea of what's going in there. Over."

"Yes, sir," Peters confirmed. "On it now. Over."

"Also," Logan continued, "compile a list of all the license plates and vehicles here in the parking lot and any parked on the street in front. Run 'em. I want to know who's in there and who's –"

"We have some movement here in front!" Peters reported. "Over."

"Steady," Logan said. "Hold steady. Do not discharge your weapons unless fired upon! Over."

The movement reached the door. The large man and father who'd absorbed the back of Jones' hard shoe, came out back first, dragging a body with an open wound showing deep burgundy blood all the way down his chest. The big man laid the corpse down gently and turned slowly to face the police line. His eyes darted back and forth. He held one hand up, and the other deliberately drifted down to his pocket. He slipped out a paper envelope slowly and brought it upward. He showed it for safety's sake and then bent down and laid it on the body. Then he self-consciously walked back inside the bank. After a moment, the speakers blared again.

"Twenty meters back. I will not ask again. We are The Unicorn!" Jones said before cutting off the mic.

Officer Peters was taken aback.

"The Unicorn?" he muttered. "What the fuck is this?"

He picked up the radio to report.

"We have a body that was just placed on the sidewalk here, Captain. The victim looks to be Middle Eastern. Also, there's an envelope. Um, should we –"

"All vehicles," Captain Logan announced, "shall retreat 20 yards away from the bank. Right now. Dispatch? We need any info available on... on The Unicorn. It looks like they may have ties to the Middle East and... This is bad."

He wiped his brow. Things were escalating past the point of uniformed officers and straight into a Homeland Security debacle.

"Peters? Carefully check it out first but get me that envelope! Over."

Logan led the charge, in reverse, to back his car up to the edge of the parking lot. The rest of the vehicles did so slowly. One officer at the wheel, the other outside using the door as cover and walking in retreating steps to stay on careful observation. Once they expanded the perimeter, Logan went back to the radio.

"Run this up the flagpole, but I think we need to get the Feds down here on this."

Just saying that felt like he was putting down a massive weight as he clicked the radio into the receiver.

"Fuck me..."

The chain of command is linked higher than most people know. That brings with it the structural and political weight of so many other branches and departmental organizations that decision-making quickly moves beyond the control of the officers on the ground. The LAPD's Commissioner was the most significant link in that chain, and the first step to getting her involved was through her assistant, Jeff Randall.

Randall was stuck in the morning LA traffic, with more than half his commute spent between other stopped vehicles and his electric car shut off while waiting for self-centered drivers in the turning lane to let him through.

He got a call and fed it through his phone into the Bluetooth-connected speaker.

"Jeff Randall," he answered. "Go."

"Mr. Randall," Michelle said, still nervous from her previous interaction just minutes before. "This is Michelle Sommers. I'm a floater -."

"Yeah, I interviewed you," he said. "You're new. Why are you calling me?"

"The Commissioner wanted me to tell you there's a bank robbery in progress out in Toluca Lake. One hostage – an Arab man, they think – has been killed. The robbers have demands, and our guys want to know if they should call in the Feds. They're saying the robbers could be terrorists –"

"Wait," he interrupted. "Terrorists? Geez... Get me everything on this situation yesterday! I'll be there in less than 10 minutes."

"Should I –."

"No," he insisted, predicting her question before she could ask. "Do not disturb Commissioner Kennedy and the Feds are not to be contacted. Tell them I said to get a Negotiator there... a man, in case these guys are–"

"Middle Eastern, yessir," she said. "On it."

"Get me that demand list," he said. He hung up and turned to the traffic on all sides. "The fuck..."

He made the call. Things would be handled without Homeland or any other boundary overstepping the LAPD. If they couldn't handle this kind of situation, what was the point of having an official elected, and what was the point of the assistants they hired?

Chapter 7

Sheila was on to phase two. All the way from across town to the penthouse corner offices of Stevenson, Gold & Drew. She was in casual clothes now – business casual, but not formal - and was about to march straight up to fulfill her next role. Stepping off the elevator, she was stunned partially by the appearance of the distractingly gorgeous receptionist. She looked up through her eyelids to God.

"Why you testing me?" Sheila whispered.

She licked her lips to get them glossy and stepped forward with a big hip swing as she walked with an envelope in hand. The receptionist finished her call and looked up to just barely meet Sheila's gaze.

"How YOU doing?" Sheila asked.

She corrected her tone and handed the envelope over.

"Look - get that to Mr. Gold as soon as possible, please."

"Will he know –."

"Paying bills," Sheila interrupted. "I'm just paying a bill. Man, I – I gotta - if I didn't have somewhere to be."

She pointed with her thumb and then started walking backward toward the elevators.

"I'll make sure," the receptionist said.

Sheila nodded. She was tempted but knew too much was at stake for her to take time making these kinds of moves. She shook her head and left.

The receptionist smiled over the sudden interaction, a pleasant break from the usual, just as the phone rang again. She set the envelope aside and picked it up to answer the call.

...

Lisa locked down the street-side doors. She obscured the glass pane with flags of the bank's name or insignia from one hinge to the other. And further with some trash cans and folders along the foot-level window area. No sightlines meant fewer control options for the cops.

57

Once she was done, she hustled over to Jones and Jimmy on the teller side of the bank. They were already dealing with cash in small stacks, ordered on top of a file cabinet while Jimmy looked over their schedule.

"Is that it?" Lisa asked.

"For phase one," Jones confirmed. "Got a way to go yet. Let's amp it up. We're set in the break room?"

She nodded.

"Are the barrels ready?"

"Handled," she confirmed. "In the bathroom closest to the street, as you said."

"Okay," Jones said. "Get the plastic bag out of my duffel and drop it in one of the barrels. Then pay a little visit to our holding areas."

Lisa nodded and took off on her rounds.

Jones looked over to Jimmy. The young man was in a deep sweat, beyond any form of acting.

"Looks like you could use a break," Jones whispered.

"No, I'm good," Jimmy said. "Not yet. I'm okay."

Jones checked Jimmy over with a quiet, analytical glare.

"Any weakness they see hurts us. Yes?"

Jimmy nodded and straightened his back. Jones patted him on the shoulder.

"Good man. Let's bring the little girl's mother first."

Jimmy nodded and went to the conference room where the customer hostages were detained. Jones watched him go. He was moving straight, but slowly although steadily. He took out his microphone to announce demands to the police again.

"We need food and drinks for 30 people and several electronic toys. We want the toys first, and we want them within 10 minutes—from the electronics store up the block – still in their boxes. There are restaurants nearby, so 30 minutes is not unreasonable. Do not deviate."

The officers heard the demands and exchanged looks. Peters picked up the walkie to confirm his action.

"What should I –"

"Go," Captain Logan said. "And no bugs. They're smart; not enough time." He sighed.

Things were starting to spiral in a way the police alone couldn't handle.

"Dispatch. What's the word from above? Where's our fucking back-up?"

• • • •

THE PHONE RANG IN THE Studio City apartment. Between each ring, the scenes of Gus' dream recall changed. First, he was with his son Jaylen, in a time when he remembered being close enough to give his then three-year-old a hug. Right in front of two teachers and the headmistress of his son's East Coast preschool.

"Oh, look how big you've gotten!" Gus said.

"Daddy!" Jaylen exclaimed.

"Promised I'd see your new school before you started kindergarten!" he said.

He rubbed Jaylen's head proudly while his son cheered. Then he felt his smile get snatched away. He went from a cool, mellow-lit room to a blindingly bright New York hotel lobby on the evening of that same day. His son and his teachers were gone and were now replaced by a cop.

"A restraining order!?" Gus snapped. "For hugging my kid?"

"Temporary," the cop assured him. "Look, I know how these things sometimes go –."

"For attempted kidnapping? Kidnapping? His teachers were right there!" Gus said.

"Mr. Martin," the cop interrupted, "I'm not taking you in as a professional courtesy. But your ex filed it so -"

"More Court bullshit. Now I don't get my scheduled visitation - even though I've got credible witnesses?" Gus said with barely restrained anger.

The cop could only shrug apologetically as he handed the papers over. A loud, rumbling chime echoed in Gus' head as he grabbed them. He couldn't read them but knew what they said. The room turned misty and dark, and he heard a distant, digitally distorted voice from the lagging connection. He turned and saw a foggy light from the screen of what looked to be a small computer.

"Pick - da - pick meeeee...."

It was a faint sound, young and scared. Gus approached the screen. It was a tablet mounted on a hunched-over desk. Jaylen was on the other side of a Skype call, and the connection made it hard to see him. Yet it was real enough that Gus felt like he could reach right through and pluck the boy up like he was a tiny puppy.

"Daddy? Come pick me up. Pick me up, okay?"

Audio samples mashed and combined together from Gus' memories.

"Come pick me up, Daddy. Daddy? I go with you, okay?"

Then the screen itself was taken away. Gus reached out for it and found himself clutching open air in the direction of his phone.

He was disoriented. He had to remember where he was and what he did. A few seconds passed until he realized what was going on. Another god-awful dream cut short multiple times from internal frustrations and external trauma. He reached for his phone and picked it up with a groggy voice.

"Yeah?"

"Rise and shine, hotshot," Captain Powell declared.

Her voice woke him up the rest of the way, and he tilted himself into a straight-up position.

"Got another situation in your zone. It's a biggie. At Vista National Bank in Toluca Lake. Clean yourself up and get over there ASAP." Captain Powell declared.

"What do we got?" he asked. "Couldn't get away with the money?" Gus asked.

"Not sure," she assessed. "They've killed at least one civilian already, maybe two. Could be terrorists. I don't know. It's a rough day today."

He shook his head and balanced his forehead in his hand.

"Yeah. Yeah, okay. I'm up. I'm on -."

"Clean up," she insisted. "There'll be news coverage on this. Detective?"

"Yeah," he said. "Okay, I will."

He hung up, forwent the formalities, and prepared himself for a date with the media in between doing his job.

Meanwhile, the number of cops on the scene were only growing. The streets, either direction, were locked down and blocked off. The media would be getting into position soon with establishing shots of the bank. The news would quickly be circulating the story across LA county, then the state, and if things lasted much longer, things would likely reach a national level.

Add to that the unpredictability of social media, and a storm was brewing.

"Let's move!" Captain Powell declared after realizing she'd been hung up on.

"It's broad daylight for Chrissakes." She looked up at the sky. "In broad daylight...."

It wasn't even noon yet. Hell, it was barely 11:30 am.

...

Douglas had just wanted to check his balance before payday to make sure he could take Chris and Zoey out to dinner that evening. He just wanted to see if things would go well this time because they'd been going so badly for so long. He had no idea he'd be the go-to accomplice for a group of murderous bank robbers. And he'd given up his gun to let them do it.

He peeked into the manager's office, where the kids were all being kept. His kids and the one other girl were, thankfully, being kept safely away from the rest of the madness. He had to conclude that the robbers were, at the very least, not total monsters. But that meant they also weren't crazed or desperate. It meant they were professionals, and, as a random citizen, he had zero chance of successfully resisting and keeping his kids safe. He could only choose one or the other.

He slipped his head just inside the door with Lisa and her gun on his back out of the children's view just in case he tried to do anything out of order.

"What you watching, baby?" he asked.

Zoey turned away from the monitor and sighed at him. She was sad but hiding it. She didn't know just how dangerous things were; she was frustrated.

"Cartoon Network, Daddy. It's on all the time."

"Really?" Douglas nodded, trying to maintain a positive face. "How about you, Chris? You need anything?"

Chris' eyes were focused and flickering around a new tablet's screen that was engaging him with some kind of video game.

"Hm?" he absent-mindedly acknowledged. "Uh-uh. I'm good."

"That's enough," Lisa whispered. "Wrap it up."

"Okay, guys," Douglas said. "I'll check back on you in a bit."

He stepped back and closed the door. All three of them, including the other little girl, seemed content, if a bit distant. Chris was the oldest at ten. He knew the difference between a bank robbery and a bad transaction. But he was still too young to have been in a situation that taught him what a dead body looked like. Douglas hesitated because there was much, he wanted to say but couldn't articulate under the circumstances. Consequently, he got poked in the back by Lisa's little attention getter... reminding him to move forward.

"Let's get you back," she insisted. "Hands."

Douglas put his hands behind his back. Lisa zip-tied them together with plastic restraints, strong enough to hold unless he did something drastic and easily visible, which he wouldn't dare do. She pushed him forward out of the small hallway and into the teller area, right past Jones. Douglas kept his eyes to the floor spitefully, but he couldn't help but catch just a glimpse of the mastermind and noticed how something about his face seemed 'off.'

...

The exterior of the scene was converted into a police encampment. It was the second one Gus had driven into within a 24-hour span and only separated by a few hours. He wasn't sure if it was a record worth bragging about. His shower kept him awake for the drive over, but he needed to quickly down an energy drink to make it the rest of the way. He sat in a black tent with Captain Logan, Officer Peters and communication specialist Carolyn Danson with a few other officers on standby outside to review the situation's briefing.

Once he got the whole gist, he was left with some questions.

"And there's absolutely nothing on these guys? Nobody knows who or what The Unicorn is about? Danson?" Gus said.

He turned to her. She just stared ahead blankly with pursed lips.

"Well shit, me neither."

He leaned forward and cradled his head, thumbs pinching the bridge of his nose.

"Okay... so we've got no video? No video. Let me see the list." Gus said.

He read the demands over.

"News reporters... Guantanamo Bay prisoners... wants to speak with the President?"

The corners of his mouth ascended as his eyes scrolled downward, and he had to laugh.

"Yeah, okay. This is bullshit. These guys aren't Jihadists."

"How do you know?" Danson asked.

"Jihadists don't negotiate," Gus explained. "Ever. Where's the phone?"

Peters handed him the designated cell phone. "I taped the phone number on the front door."

"We got eyes on the building?" Gus asked.

"On it now," Danson said. "I've put cameras on both entrances and blind spots coverage. Should be on-screen here any second."

Officer Peters continued.

"We're still getting registration info on the cars in the lot, but it looks like between bank employees and non-employees, there are at least 20, 25 people on the inside. Couple of kids, maybe."

"Two kids?" Gus asked.

Peters shrugged. "Child safety seats in some of the cars."

"Ah."

Captain Logan piped up. "We got a lot of eyes on this," he said.

"So don't fuck it up, right?" Gus said as Logan continued.

"I didn't mean – Aw, for crying out loud! Who hurt your little feelings?'

"I get it - you don't want me here. 'Above you' wants me here." Gus said.

"You sure this is a good time for you?" Logan asked.

"Deal with it –" Gus challenged before continuing "Me?"

"—and do your job, you self-righteous –." Logan said.

"My job record is –." Gus said.

Both suddenly stopped sniping. Gus was losing his cool and went quiet first. But Captain Logan decided to continue.

"Let's talk about *your* job record!"

"You don't know nothing about me!" Gus exclaimed. "And you don't get to judge anything about me either you–"

"Gentlemen," Peters shouted. "GENTLEMEN!"

The two officers went quiet, but their eyes still shot heated glares that upped the temperature of the tent.

"I'm sorry, sirs, but –."

"No, you're good, Pete," Gus said. "I just gotta try to get back the ground that's been given up already."

Logan fumed at him and sat back in his seat. Ancient history loomed.

Gus took a calming breath and cooled back down. Negotiation was all about controlling emotions and conversations. But when it came to his peers and his supposed allies, he always let himself slip and his principles lapse. He didn't keep it up with them. Better to snap at someone he worked with who knew he was capable than at someone he needed to build trust with at gunpoint.

"Look," Gus began in a moderate tone. "We're on the same team. Now... do we all understand that this is my show?"

No objections.

"I'll take that as a yes. Nobody on the roof. No choppers directly overhead. Check the sewer lines. We're right near the freeway, and I don't want anybody getting away by going underneath us. Captain, I'll leave SWAT back-up positioning to you, but they don't move unless I say. Understood?"

Logan nodded begrudgingly.

The lighting changed as Danson's screen switched views.

"We're up!" she declared.

"I'm going in," Gus confirmed. "Stevie Pete? What's the move?"

"Front door," Peters confirmed. "Separates you from our little Camp set-up back here. New beginning, maybe?"

"I like it," Gus said.

He turned to Danson.

"You got ears on this?"

He held up his cell phone. She nodded. He pointed down to the list.

"Let's get these three reporters over here with their crews. The first one here gets priority. The Unicorn wants publicity? Let's give 'em some publicity. Alright, time to rescue these hostages."

Gus walked out of the tent, through the back parking lot, and around the side street of the bank. He nodded to the officers on guard along the way. A few of them had just seen him earlier that morning; others acknowledged his presence and importance to what was going down. He pulled out his pendant and kissed it for luck, a blessing, whatever might help, and walked right around to the front door.

Looking past the front doors to the small, dark, burgundy bloodstain on the sidewalk from the corpse. Hell of a thing. He knocked on the glass door a few times and stepped way back. He held his arms wide out and held onto the designated cellphone in plain view.

"Okay," he whispered. "Here we go...."

A crowd had gathered. It was the most exciting and dangerous event in Toluca Lake in a long, long time, and it was beginning to attract all kinds from all over. Even people from neighboring quasi-cities like North Hollywood, Burbank, and Sherman Oaks were starting to come down with nothing better to do than rubberneck and be part of the scene.

Also in this growing crowd was Bird, arriving at the scene of a crime he helped cause. He blended in with his California-casual attire and sidled up near a stranger.

"You know what's going on?" he asked, as if he didn't already know.

Chapter 8

The first LA news network to pick up the growing story was ABC-7, but there wasn't any factual information to report.

Yet.

The LA Bureau office of CNN was in a regular, business-as-usual rush. Semi-panicked interns fled from desk to desk, through halls and office spaces, to get their work done to get their info to the senior reporters. It was intense, but 'normal' intense. In fact, some interns were busier beating their personal bests on their cellphone video games instead of answering the steadily ringing phones for CNN. But one did finally relent from his unofficial downtime break and actually answered a call.

"CNN Los Angeles...She's not available may I take — She's in a meeting and —. Y-yes, sir. Yessir!"

He put the call on hold and joined the rest of the panicked interns in the run-around.

He ran for a conference room, where there was already an intense discussion going on between a diverse team of elevated, long-ago interns turned reporters, producers, and production assistants attempting to make their best effort to decide what was news and what was filler. And more importantly, what would air. The intern approached just as their conversations were heated between Danielle, Mike, Steve, Fat Mike, and Hunter.

"—and why in the hell would you not report it?"

"Oh, I don't know - because he was chaos and lies last month, last week, again yesterday –."

"Alleged lies, big man. But all his actions and behavior do affect everything else –."

"Exactly - Wait -," Danielle paused. "Oh, come on, only if you're lazy or completely misinformed.

"The fuck does THAT mean?"

"Wow. Cursing, Hunter?" Steve sarcastically chastised. "Unprofessional as shit."

Fat Mike then chimed in, "Malcolm X said that '...cursing is the attempt of the feeble-minded to become forceful.'"

"I don't give a fuck –."

"Nobody gives a fuck."

"—like a Goddamn train schedule, this one," said Hunter holding in his laughter.

Steve, the calmest, piped up the loudest.

"It's like we're all stuck in that 'Ground Hog Day' movie and," he pointed to Fat Mike, "he's uh – Chris, uh..."

The intern finally made his way in, and all eyes - and all the ire and confusion - fell onto him.

"Please tell me you're quitting," Mike insisted.

"Uh," he began, swallowing to catch his breath. "There's a robbery, bank, in progress right now."

Silence, for just a moment. Then Hunter spoke up. "Well, why are you -"

"The robbers," he continued, "Have like 20 something hostages, a dead guy, and they're Middle Eastern –."

"Hostages?" Danielle asked excitedly. "Where?"

"No. The robbers," he corrected uncertainly. "Here. Well, Toluca Lake. Group called The Unicorn."

Fat Mike got up first. "Oh, I'm on this like a -."

"Shotgun, big man," Mike added.

"They want," the intern continued, "demanded – that Shelly cover it."

And they all looked to her.

Suddenly, she was the main focus. This, after sitting out the rest of the uproar on the fringes. She smiled nervously because an unexpected spotlight was suddenly, brightly, and positively on her.

"Uh, okay," she said.

Cell phones came out. Hunter was already scrolling through the web.

"At least one guy dead -."

And so was Danielle. "Where'd you get that?"

"Get me," Shelly said, "everything on The Unicorn, like, yesterday -."

The intern gulped. He still had more to say, and there was hardly any air left in the conference room to breathe, let alone fill.

"They said if you aren't there by 12:15 that -."

"Fuck!" Shelly exclaimed. "Steve, you're up. Fat Mike, Mike -."

"Wow," Danielle said, "Really?"

"Get a truck and head out!" Hunter demanded. "I gotta run all of this by Legal and the big Boys upstairs before we put jack-shit on the air."

The intern left ahead of Shelly, Mike, Fat Mike, and Steve, who ended up passing him on their way to the exit, leaving the rest of the room and Danielle, especially, feeling 'less than.'

The seconds were ticking down. It was close to their mark. Set by terrorists or not, they had a deadline to fulfill. And while they were leaving, the situation continued to expand.

Gus remained outside. He saw feet moving around inside, the bottom of what looked to be an automatic rifle, yet damage to the surroundings appeared minimal. Which meant either the rifle hadn't been used, or he had to be a crack shot at nailing a man, dead center, twice during a panic.

He waited, arms out, until his cellphone rang. It was tapped, which was exactly the point. Everyone listened in as the negotiations began. Still outdoors, he took the call and slowly brought it to his face.

"This is Lt. Martin," he began. "I am the chief negotiator and in charge of these proceedings."

The voice that came through was modulated with a distorter. The police couldn't discern the authentic voice, and to that point, they had to focus to understand what the terrorist was saying.

"You've seen our demands?" Jones asked.

"I have," Gus confirmed, "and I can assure you -."

"What we are not going to do, Gus," Jones said with a mildly condescending tone added to the name, "is lie to one another and waste time. We have what you want, and you have what we need. We demand honesty and a reasonable level of cooperation."

Gus nodded silently before responding.

"And I am interested in resolving this situation without further loss of life. As such, the release of the prisoners from Guantanamo Bay that you listed –"

"Is taking longer than expected?" Jones interrupted.

Gus hesitated.

There were procedures in order, and beat cops, and tactical units from LA didn't have the necessary connections to fulfill these kinds of demands.

"No. That's something I do not have the capability nor sufficient rank to accomplish." Gus said.

"No!?" Officer Peters exclaimed from the thrown-together central command tent. "Even I know you should never say no!"

His commentary was not fed through the line. They were on the listening end only, and he wouldn't dare call out loud enough to be heard.

Gus knew that as well, but he was the expert on the field. The job was down to him, and he knew the game and how the rules shifted depending on circumstances known and probable, most likely situations unseen.

"And the call from your President?" the robber asked.

Peters chimed in on Gus' earpiece. "Say you're working on it!"

"The President of the United States," Gus explained, "has no reason or desire to speak with any ranking member of the LAPD—including myself. He's not going to make a phone call to –"

"The Unicorn?" Jones said.

Gus looked up. The second story of the two-story structure was unoccupied. Noted.

Inside, Jones stuck two fingers in the air and signaled to one of the four workers in light blue jumpsuits. He pointed toward the cluster of blind-folded bank employees sitting on the ground behind the teller glass.

"Perhaps you are the man we need to speak with after all."

Again, Gus nodded – his way of pacing himself.

"It's my understanding that there are many people inside with you. As a show of good faith, will you consider releasing some of them?"

"Our faith is not what's being tested today, Lieutenant," Jones replied. "Continue being authentic, do your job, and perhaps we'll all get what we want."

Without another word, he hung up. Seconds later, the front door was unlocked. There was no remote locking control on the doors of this historic building. So, there was no means to keep dangerous people out or in. Just double-paned glass doors.

Hearing the lock being turned, Gus defensively stepped back a few feet, and two people exited with their hands zip-tied behind their backs.

Gus noted that they were dressed like employees of the bank branch.

Gus held up his hand for them to stop before they got out into the street.

"You're doing great," he said, "but I need you to trust me."

First looking at each other, the two freed hostages nodded their understanding and stood in place.

Gus signaled the officers to start moving in, specifically from the K9 unit. Two dogs came by and sniffed the released hostages for bombs. One of the two cringed a bit as the dogs circled them. Satisfied that there were no dangerous explosives, the dogs returned to their handlers, wagging their tails.

Officers swept in rapidly to bring the freed hostages through the police line and around to the expanding police base camp in the rear.

"Two out," Gus whispered to himself. "Good. Now... how do you know my name?"

He looked back at the bank's doors. He hid his stern, curious glare so the robbers couldn't see it. It was likely most of the hostages couldn't see a thing.

Inside, the office cubicles were repurposed into makeshift prisons for the bound and blindfolded. Even the older man, Mr. Henry, was restrained and no longer free to act out. It wasn't just his life in the balance. It was also Angela, the little children, a few more bank employees on the teller side, and every single one of the customers still inside the bank.

Angela and Patricia were bound up with several other customers, including Reese, Kevin, and Kana, who were all supposed to be somewhere else by now, doing different things that morning and still holding expectations that their day would be 'normal.' Most had on blindfolds of some type or another, but not all.

Incredibly, their whole lives were upended and tied together because they'd all had 'banking' to do that morning and because they hadn't delayed themselves by a day or even a couple of hours, here they all were.

Reese craned his head around briefly. "Anybody keep their phone?" he whispered. No answer. The silence was almost intentionally pronounced. "Just a question," he mumbled.

"A dumb one," Mr. Henry uttered.

"Look here, Pops," Reese said, turning his blind self in Mr. Henry's rough direction, "I'm not the one."

"Hey," Angela hushed, "Think! We gotta remain calm."

"Right," Kevin said sarcastically. "Ignore the guns."

"That one guy," Kana mentioned, with her blindfold askew, "he not can shoot."

"What? What is she saying?" Kevin whispered.

"Come on, man," Reese said. "Chill with all that."

"What? She has an accent."

"She said -."

"I say," Kana reiterated, "his aim bad. I saw. He kill the man but he try to shoot little girl's mom. Her."

Even though nobody else could see, Kana reflexively nodded toward Patricia, who squirmed uncomfortably due to the invisible attention she was receiving.

"Not too sure about that," Mr. Henry mentioned. "I'm a Vet, and one thing I know? That bastard knows guns." He shook his head shamefully. "The hell are they doing?"

Indeed. That was the question on everyone's mind. What was The Unicorn doing, and what were their plans for the people now being held hostage? What do they want? Most importantly, would they kill again?

They all knew that something else was going on. But what?

Chapter 9

The two freed hostages-turned-witnesses were taken behind the bank, far away from the crowd, so they could be interviewed separately. The chance, however minimal, existed that they were agents of the terrorists, sympathizers, or somehow involved in a grander plot that had to be assessed and double-checked through their stories and background data. Things wouldn't be crystal clear for quite some time, and those witnesses were barred from any outside intervention while questioning proceeded.

This was an unfortunate circumstance for the CNN crew, led by Shelly, who had just arrived at a stonewall of police refusals.

Gus showed up at the perimeter and waved them through.

"They're okay," he called. "Hey, let them through!" He ducked his head into the counselor's tent. "Separate the two and start getting descriptions of everybody they can remember. Everybody."

The lead counselor nodded and returned to his duty. He drew the tent shut and prepared the advanced questioning while Gus followed through on his part with the demands. He walked up to the reporters.

Shelly took the initiative. "Hi. Shelly Reyes, CNN. They said you were Lieutenant –."

"Right," he said. "Gus Martin. Lead negotiator for... this."

He pointed over his shoulders to the scene at his rear.

"Gus Martin," she said. "I know that name."

"I doubt it," he said. "Look, I don't know how you got on these guys' radar or why, but this is not the place to get cute or get exclusive inside whatever. You got me?"

Shelly looked taken aback, unsure if she should signal for the camera or the mic or just let it ride out as a warning. Gus could tell she struggled to process him and slowed down a bit.

"I'm not coming down on you, but I need you to understand that you're here because they demanded it. But you must follow my orders because anything you do can cost people their lives. Alright?"

He waited for a nod, but time was ticking down, and he could feel the moments slipping away. "I just hope you're not thinking about awards here. Stay back. Follow instructions. Do your job."

He pointed to the far end of the parking lot.

"Get your team, set 'em up over there. I'll see about getting you guys a tent."

"Got it," she replied. "Where can I get info that will bring me up to speed, Lieutenant? Since I'm here and my presence was demanded?"

Now Gus was the one who needed to catch up as Shelly continued.

"We won't get in your way, but I am not gonna sit around with my thumbs in my ass. There's a story here!"

"You're right," he conceded. "And part of your job is to help me figure out why they want you to tell it."

Gus walked away to return to his job while Shelly's team reunited with her in her heated state. She had plenty of words to say, not all good, about her situation. She thought she came to get a first-hand account of a modern-day bank heist event but was being relegated to sideshow duty instead.

"He in charge?" Fat Mike asked.

"In charge? Yeah," she said. She turned to see the other two still at the van, gathering gear. "Get Research to find out what Lt. Gus Martin's deal is."

"What?" Fat Mike said.

She answered him with a flat stare that resonated deeper than the question required but not the moment.

"Right. On it."

Fat Mike pulled out his phone and headed back to the van while Shelly got over to their designated area.

Gus heard the designated cell phone go off and turned to Logan. He gave a signal to listen in to the call and answered.

"Lt. Martin," he greeted.

Jones was on the other line, voice still modified but more intelligible. "Tell your new friend to be ready to go on-air on the hour, Gus."

Gus checked his watch. "Wait, 37 minutes? To do what?"

"Remember," Jones said. "You being cooperative gets us both what we want."

"Mutual cooperation," Gus mentioned. "Let me see what's going on in there. Just me."

Jones paused and thought it through. The silence was palpable.

"Front door," he said. "In three minutes." He hung up. Gus waved for Logan to come over and started walking in Shelly's direction. Logan caught up with Gus shortly after.

"I heard," he said. "What's the plan?"

"You heard the man," Gus said. "I'm going in. Bigger issue... He's got eyes back here somewhere. Can your guys lowkey look for cameras? Don't move 'em. I just want to know where the fuck they are."

Logan turned to leave but quickly turned back to perhaps continue their earlier argument.

"Logan, look," Gus spoke out first, "I don't want to go back and forth –."

"Forth with me?" Logan continued. "Do you want to know where the cameras are or not?"

Gus was chagrinned but nodded affirmatively.

"Don't look now," Logan said, "but all the exterior cameras are pointed at–."

"This way," Gus said. "Oh, this motherfucker here. Good spot."

He stopped and pretended to look at his watch but was side-eyed to see a camera over the ATMs facing away from the bank before turning back to Logan.

"Favor? Tell Shelly what's-her-name she's on in 35minutes. I gotta head up front."

"You got it," Logan said. "Hey, use the phone."

Gus nodded, glad they seemed to be on the same page for a change and walked around to the front of the bank. He waited, ready for the doors to be unlocked to allow him entry. A measure of trust, even if it felt like a trap.

"So, you want to play games," he muttered....

...

City Hall's agenda moved from department budgets and administrative woes to the breaking news of the Toluca Lake robbery in progress. Jeff Randall was on the scene and power-walked through the halls to his office. The Commissioner was not present, but four administrative assistants worked in nearby cubicles of the common area. Jeff cleared his throat to break their concentration for a moment and turned their focus to him.

"Good morning, everyone. Commissioner Kennedy will likely be in meetings all day, and several things are important. Please let me know immediately about anything with any heat. Any calls requesting interviews with the Commissioner or anything new on the hostages in Toluca Lake should be forwarded to my cell ASAP. Be great today; we're counting on you."

With that, he entered his office to start the long day. It still wasn't even noon.

...

Douglas opened the door to the bank. He moved very rigidly and specifically, adhering to the exact instructions he was given. He locked eyes with Gus as he approached and whispered to him as he passed.

"There's three kids," he warned, "in the manager's office. Two are mine!"

Gus nodded as he walked, like a bob of his head, and entered the bank. Douglas closed the doors again and lowered his whole head to keep his eyes on the floor. Gus was on their turf, on their terms.

He scanned the situation. Far across the lobby, near the back doors, was, who he guessed, the main perpetrator. He appeared to be an imposing man with an uninteresting face, wispy gray hair, and pale skin. He had his rifle up at Gus. Gus noticed notches in the wall - height markings behind him at the rear entrance.

"That's close enough," Jones insisted.

"No weapons," Gus said, hands out and belt bare. "See?" He waved the phone in his hand to keep attention up on it. "Just our personal walkie-talkie. I just want to make sure everybody's doing okay."

"Keep your hands where I can see them," Jones commanded.

Gus pulled his hands up slowly, as though he was being robbed.

"We talked about not lying to each other. Remember that, Gus?"

"I remember," Gus nodded.

"You're here," Jones assessed, "to view the hostages, see how many of us there are and to determine if we're stable or if maybe we're crazy."

"And," Gus added, "you're gonna tell me that I can see everything I need to see from where I'm at right now."

Jones tilted his head to the side but kept the rifle trained on him.

Gus turned his upper body to the right to peek into the conference room on the personal banking side. Just inside the door, he saw several customers bound and blindfolded, seated on the floor. To the left, behind the glass and the teller stands, were employees clustered together similarly except out in the open.

"This everybody?" Gus asked.

"Not quite," Jones said. "The truth is what we're after. As long as we get the truth, you'll get what you want."

"And The Unicorn?" Gus asked. "What's that about?"

"Do you believe in Unicorns, Lieutenant?"

Gus was trained to be receptive to unreasonable demands, wild ideas, and stressful, emotionally driven lapses of logic. Being asked a question like that wasn't enough to throw him off balance as he correctly perceived it was meant to do. At that moment, he assessed the hostage taker as a gamer - someone who had an objective beyond the apparent and wanted to enlighten the people who were sent to dull his efforts. He was honest, even in his seemingly maniacal efforts.

"As long as nobody else gets hurt," Gus confirmed.

"Well," Jones said, with a pause, "then you have a lot of responsibility. FOUR!"

The sudden shout made Gus tense up. He wasn't sure to expect four shots, or four of something else. Thankfully, it was four hostages. Carmelita, Ronald, and two other employees were sent out from a room behind the clustered employees to Gus.

"Good faith gesture, right?" Jones said. "It's almost show time."

Gus nodded, slow and deep, in a nearly thankful half-bow.

Jones motioned to Douglas, who remained behind to work the door, which he then opened. The hostages filed out ahead, and Gus stepped backward with his hands still up, taking in the last bits of visual information, slowly leaving until he was back outside in front of the bank.

Douglas sealed the doors as Gus walked with the newly freed employees and then -.

Two gunshots.

Startled, Gus jumped. The whole police line went quiet for a moment. Quiet orders circulated. The news crew all turned with brightened eyes toward the bank. Gus' phone rang. He picked it up with a snap.

"You recorded video on your phone without my permission," Jones declared, "so another innocent life is lost."

Gus gritted his teeth. He was sure the gambit wasn't discovered. He wasn't sure what gave it away. The phone wasn't showing anything when they recorded it for a test earlier. It was either a bluff or a lark. Still, on the call, Gus began walking again until...

Douglas exited from the bank under the scrutinous iron sights of about a dozen guns with another body, another man dead, and another envelope. He looked up apologetically and returned inside the bank, nearly crawling as he slipped just out of sight.

"I showed good faith, Gus, but how we proceed from here is up to you. Top of the hour. Don't be late." He hung up.

Gus jogged back to get the envelope from the body and turned to Stevie Pete at the front line.

"Get two officers to help with this man," he shouted. "Now, Officer Peters!"

Gus ran back to the four employees on the side of the building, envelope in hand. He was about to read it when he felt his pocket shake. His own phone was ringing instead. For a second, he thought it was going to come from inside the bank - that the game was about to deepen even further. He was almost relieved to see that it was Captain Powell.

"Go for Gus, Captain."

"Got a body here," she reported, "at Toluca Lake, you might find interesting. Two to the chest. A Cathy O'Brien... branch manager at your bank there."

"Shit," Gus said. "At the lake. Outside?"

"Yeah," she sighed. "Broad daylight. How's it going over there?"

"It's coming," he said. "Still putting the puzzle together."

"You need me to send over any –?"

"No. I'm good," he said. "Thanks, Captain."

He hung up and turned to see the body being carried around. Deep red right in the chest. And he recalled the briefing he received - two in the chest of the Middle Eastern man, his shirt dampened with dark red by the time anyone got the body out of the way.

Two shots then, two shots at the lake, two just now.

Pairs, twos, duos, links - his mind started churning like an investigator's naturally would. He needed to figure out how to talk to the maniac behind those frosted glass doors....

Chapter 10

Typically, City Hall was abuzz, though not with local news. Their focus was usually more widespread across many cities and counties in the much broader LA county area. The priorities of upper management and administration were rooted in problems and politics instead of the most recent symptoms both continued to cause.

A not-very-exciting presenter stood in front of a projector screen showing a PowerPoint laden with graphs, charts, and mapped areas highlighted in various shades of the same color.

"...so, this activity had started spreading across these zones whereas before it was relegated and remained stagnant..."

Commissioner Kennedy sat and took in regurgitated information passively. Jeff Randall entered discreetly, ducked along the wall to reach her, and whispered rapidly into her ear.

She turned with a start after he was done. "How many?" she asked as the room turned to stare.

"Two at the bank," he reported without bending down, "plus one more. Got twenty or so hostages with six released; all employees."

"And who!?" she exclaimed.

"The Unicorn," he reported. "Terrorists, maybe."

She turned to those in the meeting and the presenter, whose attention she'd unintentionally stolen.

"My apologies, everyone."

She stood up and purposefully walked with Randall close behind. They were off to other matters and left the presentation early.

...

Logan watched the closed-circuit transmission over Danson's shoulder and anxiously waited to meet Gus after he'd heard the shots. Gus got there a little after a minute.

"The fuck happened in there?" Logan demanded.

"The plan," Gus said, "that we agreed to. Letter by letter. But he knew. Motherfucker knew!"

He paused to wipe his forehead. Logan shook his head, upset but onboard. Gus handed him the designated phone.

"Get somebody to download the video. I need that plus clear screen grabs asap. Oh... where's the list of who these cars belong to?"

"Here," Logan handed over the list in exchange.

Now Gus' personal phone rang again as he watched two officers carry the covered body around from the front of the bank toward the triage tent, out of sight from the public. He checked his phone screen, expecting another name starting with a military call sign. Instead, it was Theo Gold's office. Gus was curious. He looked over at the four just-released employees nearby and stopped Logan from running off.

"You see if they can ID that body? I gotta take this."

Logan nodded.

Gus turned around and answered.

"Theo? Sorry, I'm a little busy -."

"Yeah. Me too," Theo said, with the slight echo indicant of a courthouse bathroom picking up in the background.

"Okay. So, I'm thinking an ex parte' order."

"Wait, what?"

"I know. It's a stretch," he began, arrogant but confident. "But keeping your kid from communicating with you could - could now - be interpreted as a distant cousin to kidnapping if we play it right."

"Uh, okay," Gus said. "If you think the judge will buy it. Thank you... so much, but I really gotta-"

"Yeah, me too." He hung up in a rush.

Gus held his phone back in shock.

"Fuck got into him?" he whispered. Another mystery was added to the pile.

Meanwhile, Captain Logan swung into his own and commenced with his duties as the most senior officer on hand. He took Ronald and Carmelita aside to start. They both had shock blankets over their shoulders, not to keep out the cold of the increasingly warm California day but to keep them feeling safe.

"Excuse me. I'm Captain Logan." He pointed over to Gus. "I work with him. Look, I know this is a lot."

"Yeah, man," Ronald nodded. "Crazy."

"Need a favor," Logan said.

"What's going on?" Carmelita asked.

Logan turned to the two cops-made coroners. "HEY, FELLAS," he called. He turned back to the two employees. "I need one or both of you to identify this body if you can. Only if you're up to it."

"No, it's fine," Carmelita said.

"Okay," Ronald agreed. "Yeah, sure."

The cops brought the body over on a stretcher and carefully pulled back the tarp that covered his face only. It was a dead, younger-looking man, about as old as either of the tellers, in casual clothing stained with a deep red.

"No," Ronald said. "Don't recognize him."

"Nope," Carmelita sighed. Then, an epiphany. "Wait!" They turned and whispered with shock. "This is one of the robbers!"

"What?" Ronald said before he took another look from a different angle. "Oh wow. Right! He had a gun."

"On the teller side wearing a jumpsuit!" Carmelita added.

Ronald glanced at them.

"Well, he was," Carmelita added with comedic authority.

Logan covered the face back up. The blanket rustled just enough to see the shirt pocket had been shot through on the way to the heart. Given everything that was happening and the speed with which it was happening, nobody noticed the blood oozing so slowly.

His personal situation miraculously moving forward, Gus returned to the group with his list, where he had his thumb pinned down under one of the names on the license plate roundup - Cathy O'Brien.

"Okay, thanks," Gus said.

Logan was about to say something to add to the compounding mystery but left to allow Gus to follow-up in his own way.

"I'm Lt. Martin, the lead negotiator on the case. Stay over there with the counselors, please. Okay? Hey! Watch these two." A counselor acknowledged and came over to take the two away.

Gus then turned to the two cops.

"Tell Danson to get a forensics team on the," he checked the list, "off-white Volvo S90 2020. I want fingerprints, receipts in the glove box, everything, and I need it now. Tell her, 'Don't fuck it up.' Thanks."

The officers acknowledged and followed their orders, starting with securing the body with the others on-site.

....

It was almost time for the big show.

But first, it was time for lunch. The hostages now had their hands in front of their bodies to eat the freshly delivered food, but each remained blindfolded. They'd been given clear instructions to leave their blindfolds in place while using their hands to grab the food from their individual rectangular white paper lunch boxes.

Jones had total reign over the lobby. He was getting hot but could feel a dry chill on his neck. Sooner or later, his makeup would start to run.

"I hope your meals are sufficient, given the circumstances. We will be re-handcuffing you in–."

He stopped next to Mr. Henry's chair, where the cranky older man stayed sitting, neither bound nor blindfolded, unlike the rest of the group. This included Angela, the only employee still out in the lobby area. It caught his eye.

"Why is *she* in here!? I told you I wanted bank employees together!"

"You let her be!" Mr. Henry snapped.

"Old man," Miguel lowed. "Why the fuck is your blindfold down?"

Mr. Henry growled at him. "Cause I need to see when I'm eating!"

"That's it," Jones said. "I've had it. Bring him."

"Don't," Angela said. She swallowed something whole to clear her mouth so she could talk. "Please, wait…"

"He's got to go," Jones demanded. "Now shut up." He paused and looked at Miguel. "Know what? Bring her too. I don't want to hear another peep out of this room!"

Jones marched out while Miguel went to work.

Angela started weeping. She dropped her sandwich to the floor and fell forward. Seeing her collapse, Miguel left her there and went to tie up Mr. Henry, but the old man swung at him with a weak, feeble drop.

"Get your hands off me! Let go!"

"Stop it!" Another woman cried out. "You're going to get us all killed!"

"Chill out!" Reese demanded. "You gotta chill -."

"Shut up!" George shouted. He stomped into the room, voice louder than a gunshot. "We will now reposition everyone's hands behind your backs!"

He pulled out a new batch of zip ties for everyone's hands. The hostages either gave up on eating or pushed the rest of their food into their mouths and assumed the positions once the front ties were cut. Miguel picked Angela up by her wrists and got Mr. Henry in a grip under his armpit.

"Let's go, Pops. You too, Move!"

He dragged them both off per Jones' command. The top of the hour was coming up…

…

Shelly held the still sealed envelope in her hand and balked at the instructions which were passed down to her by the police.

"Wait. So, we're supposed to go live, but I can't even look to see what's in here?"

Captain Logan nodded.

"That's what the instructions said. Gotta open it on-air. Plus... they got eyes out here. Don't look–"

"Where?" Mike demanded.

"Jesus," Fat Mike whispered. "What are you, seven? He just said, 'don't look.'"

"Where?" Shelly asked.

"Bank's exterior cameras are facing us," Logan said.

"No."

"Oh, the interview?" he said. "In your tent, I guess."

Shelly's mouth was agape in frustration. Gus entered and looked for Logan's attention.

"Got a minute?"

"Lieutenant," Shelly began, "what the fuck?"

"You know what I know," he said with his hands up.

Shelly rolled her eyes while Gus and Logan stepped away from the small media tent.

"What'd they say?"

"Dead guy?" Logan asked. "Two rounds in the heart. Said he's one of the robbers."

"Shit," Gus whispered.

He palmed his forehead as his head slowly rose.

"This is what they wanted," he said to himself as much as to Logan.

"What?"

"The Unicorn. They didn't fuck-up a robbery. This isn't about money. They did the first VIC and the bank manager the same way. Yeah. Did her over at the lake then drove her car here - that one."

He pointed to the Volvo on the back row where the forensics team was in the middle of a dust-down and careful search.

"I'm running it for prints and whatever else they can find."

"Okay," Logan said. "Then I'm sending my team in."

"No," Gus said. "This isn't what it looks like!"

He could tell Logan was drifting away.

"Think... Play it back. Aside from the cameras, what have I missed?" He waited for confirmation and went off the slight pout of Logan's lip. "Exactly. I'm on my fucking game, Logan. Now look, I need you with me. Not back-seat driving or second guessing. These guys are not Jihadists or some kind of whackos. They're something else, like... like suicide bombers maybe."

"Have you lost your fucking -"

"See if you can get our two bodies ID'd," Gus said. "Just you! Them, this bank manager; you'll see. They're connected."

Gus piped down just in time to hear the blaring sirens approaching in the distance. It was a whole damn motorcade. The kind that didn't drive to stop crime but used to escort the very source of all policing decisions in the LA county area.

"Sounds like we've got company. Try and stall them. I'm telling you—They are connected. When we put it together, we get all the hostages."

Logan took a hard look into Gus' eyes. There was some sleep deprivation and remnants of the tense, unresolved situation from earlier that morning. But there was a lot more sincerity and faith now. The exact things he had when he went into that apartment building, unarmed, to free a highly dysfunctional family earlier.

Logan nodded and accepted his placement in things. It was Gus' show, and he was the producer, to keep things rolling along with the rest of the crew.

Taking a deep breath to bolster himself, Logan turned to meet the motorcade as it was guided past the blockades and into the lot. A heavy Mercedes mobile command unit pulled in. The first to exit was none other than Commissioner Kennedy, followed closely by her assistant Jeff Randall.

Logan gave a parting glance to Gus, a confirmation of trust, and then began walking over to handle the new obstacle.

Chapter 11

The CNN crew was in a huddle outside their tent base. Things were going weird. It was nothing like any staged shot they'd filmed before for the sake of news. The staging was all real and very gruesome. They weren't wartime correspondents; they were LA city journalists. Worst case scenario, they would report on hearing gunshots, not being within visible proximity to them – live, no less. And in broad daylight of all things. Then there was the matter of their go-between, the one who got them involved in the first place. Their perfectly imperfect interview piece, Lt. Gus Martin.

"What do you mean?" Shelly asked. "Like he went crazy?"

"No, not crazy," Mike said. "Two Cops went down during a situation he was managing or negotiating or whatever."

"And?" Steve asked. "Shit happens. It's a dangerous job."

"Wasn't official, but people say it was his fault," Mike continued. "Like maybe he was distracted by personal stuff."

"Really?" Shelly said. She repeated to him, "Wasn't official, but people say it was his fault. That's your intel?"

"Not me," Mike said. "It's from Corporate." Shelly and Fat Mike both put the screws to him, silently. "Okay! Danielle and Hunter. They both checked him out."

"Yeah, okay," Steve said. "This camera's set for Mike. I'll run the 'B' camera out front. Fat man... get her mic'd up. Look, I trust him. Seems on the ball to me." Steve left the huddle and grabbed the 'B' camera. Fat Mike dropped the mic cord through the top of Shelly's blouse like he was threading but using her whole body as a needle. They fist bumped. Yet another action-packed scene in the making. She then grabbed his fist briefly and pulled him in closer.

"There's some skeletons in this guy's closet," Shelly said, "but there'd almost have to be with his frigging job. Shit, I just hope he doesn't freeze up when we start rolling."

"We're playing it straight, right?" he asked. She didn't answer. "Right?"

"Oh, you betcha," she confirmed. Fat Mike gave Mike a look.

"What? I'm gonna follow the instructions." She noticed the lights on the big van pulled up across the lot. "Oh, don't look now but looks like the varsity just pulled in." She watched from the far end of the parking lot as a story unfolded and captured it with her eyes. Royal chewing out from the Commissioner down onto the head of the likely office cop out of his element.

Inside, the robbery crew awaited the coming moments.

George huffed at his workstation in the break room. He had four monitors going that were all monitoring the exterior and controlled by the same mouse drag-and-tilt control scheme. Just the desk work alone seemed to provoke a sweat to kick-in. He spotted the news crew moving into position and got up to report to Jones.

"News crew looks ready," he said.

Jones looked down at George. The compassion in his eyes, the gratefulness shone, even through his mask.

"A little further, my friend."

"Yeah," George nodded. "Only thing... nobody will ever know that it was us."

"But they will remember this day," Jones said. "Let's finish this."

George nodded and exited. Jones got up and strode out of the break room and through the teller area into the lobby. The next phase was already underway.

And it was Bird's turn to act. He checked his watch. Nearly, high noon on the dot. He started weaving through the crowd, which was already restless with people moving to get a better look at the new cop cars that came in and catching glimpses of the news crew off in the far corner of the lot nearest the side street.

"Hey, did you hear about the interview?" Bird said. Then he changed to a different whisper tone, just in earshot of some people on their phones. "Yeah! I heard it was gonna start at the top of the hour."

He moved and continued, whispering like an unseen devil over people's shoulders.

"A cop back over there said it was a terrorist group... called 'The Unicorn.' Yeah. 'The Unicorn.'"

And on to the next section of the crowd, he went. "Hey, a cop told me some hostages got released. But then he said that like five or six have been shot and killed," and his rumormongering continued. "I don't know... but I heard there's an interview on CNN soon..."

Every whisper turned into a tweet, an Instagram post, a status update, a live stream taken over a dozen or more heads from dozens of yards away. Everyone wanted to be a source of information, but the reality was that most were grasping at straws for 'likes.' The media was there, and the internet was there. There was no shortage, at all, of eyes on the developing situation and no shortage of developments unfolding just out of reach.

Evelyn Kennedy was making her rounds through the base camp. She took her sweet time, which Gus knew was at a premium, as she listened to Randall inform her of more hurried, breaking developments... many retrieved from his cell phone.

"It's coming from absolutely everywhere," he softly informed her. "On every possible social media platform -."

"Enough," she demanded. "Everybody except Lt. Martin out. Give us the room—the space! Now!"

Everyone filtered out to the perimeters of the tent and then beyond, as the cloth walls were not nearly as private as they looked. Gus tried to maintain eye contact with the two hellfire comets in her skull, but he had to look back down at his watch.

"Commissioner?" he said. "We've only got six minutes -."

"Because you, Lieutenant," she began, heated but professional, "do not have control of this situation. You had the unmitigated gall to try and have Logan gaslight me? We have critical information leaks, situational rumors, and dead hostages on your watch!"

Gus took the first round of verbal beating and stayed standing.

"Commissioner, I know how this looks –."

"No," she said. "I don't think you do. You're looking at this through a microscope. I have to view it through a goddamn kaleidoscope. I am looking at everything! And the subtext of the optics, racially speaking, is just—Geezus! Why should I believe you haven't already lost those people in there, including children? Your record? Not exactly pristine. How dare you tell me how much time–"

"Commissioner?" he spoke up. "One event does not define me. You didn't get to where you are in smooth, easy steps. Fuck the optics! You know what it takes to be a negotiator? It's not just technical information. You have to have a feel! The facts we already have and the feel flowing through me scream that this was never a robbery."

"What?" she said, as though she were trying to ascertain his level of sanity. "What do you mean?"

He had her attention and refused to mince details.

"The bank, the money... it's all misdirection! I believe the people killed so far are all part of their group. They are killing themselves to make a point. Let's figure out what it is after we get the hostages. Ma'am? We're on their clock, and our time is about up."

She furled an eyebrow at him.

"So, I should just trust you?"

"No, ma'am," he said. "We need to trust each other. Especially us."

Kennedy gritted her teeth at what she knew was a coded racial remark.

"That is not what this is about," she snapped. But that didn't mean it wasn't true.

He held still, held back, and waited.

There were more barriers between them than between him and the robbers at that point. Barriers of class, gender, age, life experience, family history - too many for him to knock down in time for them to collectively trust one another in the way they needed to. Even their jobs weren't the same because he wasn't one of her cops by trade.

She twisted the wedding ring on her finger.

"And it's not why I'm saying yes." She craned her head up and raised her voice. "Clear a path for our negotiator!"

Gus exited and headed for the reporter's tent. He heard the beating of air not-quite overhead, choppers hovering within view, audible from nearly a mile away, scoping the scene from above. The crowd across the street past the barricade had half aiming their phones, and the other half's heads were turned down to type out tweets, posts and captions. It was a circus, and the cops were the clowns in The Unicorn's parade. Then -

Two gunshots.

Muffled, but still clearly there. The crowd shrieked a bit. The cops went on alert.

Seconds later, Douglas appeared with another body. This time, a woman in plain clothes, oozing dark blood out of her chest. The speakers squeaked to life.

"A television interview was supposed to begin two minutes ago. You now have three minutes before another life will be lost. We are The Unicorn."

Gus stood stock still at the scene, watching on CNN monitors as Douglas once more retreated into the bank. Thankfully, he knew that there were still no dead customers, but the world had no idea. Still, nobody he saw was tied up. The same two-shot pattern.

What does that mean?

Kennedy took to a screen with the rest of the officers to monitor the scene from the temporary command center.

"Damn it," she said, turning to Jeff. "Get me the mayor!"

He nodded and ducked his way out to make the call...

...

Jones watched from the break room monitors. Manuel sat next to him - panting.

"Okay," Jones said. "Can you go turn on the television for the group over there? They need to understand–"

"Are we doing the right thing here?" Manuel asked. His voice was still gruff as always, but his breathing was becoming too heavy.

Jones shut his eyes to gather the right words in his head.

"What we know," he explained, "is how things are done now... doesn't help the people most in need. Yes?"

Manuel nodded his head somewhat sleepily.

"No," he answered. "Not one bit."

Jones nodded with him.

"Thank you for –."

Jones hushed him with a finger against his lips. Manuel nodded and left the room. He pulled himself up along the wall and straightened his back before he headed back onto the floor. He left Jones with Angela tied up on the floor nearby. She sat quietly, blind, and doing her best to appear as though she wasn't listening.

"You've been courageous throughout this situation Miss. But now I need something special from you."

He stood up and reached behind a holster on his waist, hidden by his long jacket. He drew out a knife and let the metal sheer against the material of his shirt so she could hear it....

Chapter 12

The interview was underway.

George connected the feed and turned up the volume just as the header crossed the screen: "Toluca Lake Robbery turned Hostage Negotiation Panic."

Shelly sat next to Gus, both in frame, mic'd up and staring into the camera. Gus was a professional on his foldout canvas chair with the rear of the bank directly in front of them as Shelly continued.

"...and part of The Unicorn's demands require that I open this envelope," she waved it just in front of her shoulder, "on-camera and address its contents to Lieutenant Augustus Martin, who is the lead negotiator on this case. Lt. Martin has agreed to these terms–"

"We have negotiated these terms in an effort to successfully exchange information The Unicorn believe I have knowledge of, for the lives of the remaining..." he paused to pick the proper word carefully, knowing who all would be watching and what he wanted them to know he knew, "people still inside the bank. So far, we've been able to secure the safe release of six–"

"Hostages —."

"—*people*, all of whom are employees of the bank."

Gus shot Shelly a look, giving her a go-ahead to follow up – using his plan. She remained undaunted by his correction and tore open the envelope slowly and carefully. She did it just close enough to her mic that it picked up the sound of paper for effect. It was a single sheet of paper, plainly printed text. Gus kept his eyes on her, careful not to read it, and she was careful not to let him, exactly as instructed.

She read it over once and fought back a smirk in the dire setting.

She kept her eyes locked on the paper as she read.

"We are 'The Unicorn,' and we seek only the best for those in our circle and the truth in all things. Lieutenant... what happened at the nail shop you were called to over six months ago?"

Gus' eyes went somewhere between Shelly and the camera, a thousand miles away.

"Oh, shit," Logan muttered. He, and every other officer, were watching the interview, with only Danson still concerned about the police cameras stationed outside. Kennedy and Randall were also looking on, being part of the privy crowd.

Gus took a short, bracing breath and answered.

"There was an attempted robbery during a scheduled cash pick-up," he explained. "The nail salon was full of customers, and unfortunately... the robbers were not aware of who owned that particular nail shop."

The speakers crackled on – which startled the now much larger crowd.

"Be more specific, please," Jones announced.

Shelly held her eyes on the camera, not wanting to seem spooked by the sudden interruption that broke the carefully established fourth wall to her audience.

For Gus, it was just another voice in the conversation. The one he had to hear. The actual target of his skills, all things considered. Shelly was the Ray of this exchange. The man inside, the head of 'The Unicorn', was the new Arlene.

"Turns out the nail shop was part of a money laundering operation for a criminal syndicate who kept watchful eyes on their money. The robbers wouldn't give up the money, and the syndicate refused to let the robbers get away. Several customers were caught in the crossfire... some didn't make it. Police arrived on the scene, and I was called in to... sort things out. But when I arrived, we - I - I did not know about the syndicate or their people. I only knew about the attempted robbery, the robbers and what appeared to be a routine crisis."

Something happened in front of the bank. A haggard and clearly frightened Patricia was suddenly released – almost shoved out - and she didn't like it. Not one bit. She fought to get back inside by pounding on the doors.

"Wait! No! No!" she wailed.

Shelly stared at the monitor showing Mike's B-Camera vantage.

"As you can see," she reported, "one of the hostages has just been released! There seems to be some confusion as to why—"

"Get back to the interview," Gus demanded. He raised his voice. "Get back to the interview! Please."

Shelly sat back down.

"Of course, of course," she said.

She believed she understood. It was theatrics. Deadly theater. Part of the instructions, unwritten, was for the other side to fulfill in exchange for Gus' words.

Stevie Pete and another officer raced forward and wrestled Patricia away from the door to take her around to central command. The crowd watched with various wrong kinds of takes as to what was happening, while many listened to the interview through earbuds or headphones as closely as they could.

Gus continued.

"After convincing two of the surviving robbers to come out with their hands up, a third attempted to slip by with a large amount of cash... and the men from the syndicate who were watching from behind our police line opened fire. Killing him... and two of our officers."

"Ah," she said, finally getting the answers she'd wanted earlier. "Now I remember that case. You were placed on suspension. What were the circumstances involved, Lieutenant? Because an internal affairs review of the case found that you—"

Two shots rang out from inside the bank - immediately causing Shelly to freeze and clearly demanding everyone's silence.

Seconds passed. The front door opened yet again, and Douglas still deposited another body, this one a gruff-looking middle-aged man with slicked back hair and blood that oozed slowly from his chest cavity area. It was Manuel. Douglas dipped his head away, avoiding the cameras, and hurried back inside the bank.

The speakers kicked on again.

"The interview will resume in exactly 10 minutes."

The official feed immediately cut back to the studio hosts. Airtime regulations forbade them from showing a real dead body, and they'd inadvertently shown three whole seconds of it – three seconds more than the F.C.C. permitted.

Back on the scene, Shelly was left in shock.

"Oh my god! Oh my god!" she panted. "I wasn't thinking. They killed that man because I–"

"Because," Gus whispered, fully in control, "you did exactly what I told you not to do. Listen... I need you to stay here in clear view of those bank cameras and turn that paper over. Stay right where you are. Do not tell anybody what is on that paper."

He turned to Fat Mike. "Get her some water."

Fat Mike helped disconnect Gus' mic and slipped it off while Gus sprinted across the lot to the command center.

Fat Mike came down to Shelly where she sat.

"You okay?"

She stammered. "I fucked-up. Walked right into it..."

The command tent was already abuzz in plenty of ways. The Commissioner was reviewing all the data that had been gathered with a keen eye, filtering out all the trash and collecting the purest grains of intel. She saw the video Gus snuck out with earlier, and a freeze frame zoomed in to where Jones was standing, back to the measuring wall.

"Jesus," Jeff said. "This guy is huge. Martin didn't say anything about -."

Gus entered.

"Give us the space, please," Kennedy said.

The whole crew departed at once.

"Okay. Your two bank employees say this last guy was another one of the robbers. How many would you say there are altogether? We need to send Logan's SWAT Team in now."

"No," he said.

"No?" she asked.

"I'm not positive how many robbers there are," he said. "I know it looks like we're losing hostages to the media, but you know that's not true."

She sighed and shook her head, remaining quiet and in control.

"But this is not a good look. You've gotta take the lead on this. Right now, the clear perception is that we're following along behind this guy. That we're not in control. Do it your way but do it. Now... give me a profile on him."

Gus nodded and got all his thoughts sorted. Things were finally moving into his arena, where his opponent had fewer pieces as time went on.

"Uh... thorough, military background - all deceased have taken two shots to the heart. Detail-oriented, knows people... how they react to pressure. Applies cerebral techniques to control thought and behaviors... to achieve desired outcomes. He's reaching for something he already knows happened at that nail shop. This guy's played this chess game a thousand times and knows our standard operating procedures."

"Ex-cop?"

"Doubt it," he said. "Hmm, maybe. But he deals with the mind. Shrink, professor, counselor –."

"Okay, let me run with that."

He nodded his agreement before she asked a question of concern.

"You, okay?"

"Yeah," he replied, almost too quickly. "Heat coming down?" he asked, trying to return the favor.

"Oh, yeah," she answered. "But keep looking through your microscope. I got your back. Let me handle the heat."

"Roger that."

Finally, reciprocal trust was being earned and acknowledged here in the command center between the two.

They were beginning to truly see one another beyond their titles and positions in a patriarchal structure created long before anybody who looked like them could even apply for employment with the LAPD. Trust begets truth, and as a result, the truth was getting closer to them.

But it was moving further from the public.

It was the greatest tour of Talking Heads since the 80s. News networks across the nation had now picked up on the story. Specifically, the part where someone was murdered live on-camera as well as live streams and deposited on the curb out front. The crowd had also become the media of sorts, and their 'not newsfeeds' blended with the actual Media's to turn truth into a cacophony of misinformation and dread-peddling for the doom-scrollers of the world.

"...but there'll be plenty of time to criticize the ineptitude of LAPD once this horrific situation is finally over."

"...and we, as a nation, never negotiate with terrorists. Yet here we are with at least four dead hostages because of doing the exact opposite. It's just a needless loss of life that terrorism experts should've handled..."

"... over 40 hostages are still being held at this time. It's not completely known what demands have been made as the police are being very secretive about the inner workings of their talks with 'The Unicorn'..."

"... which puts the hostages in further danger because they are not using military-level force against these Jihadists. Deadly force is the only thing they truly respect."

And out of CNN, a somewhat snarky Danielle was also reporting:

"... and so, one wonders whether reporter Shelly Reyes's exuberance to get a more detailed answer and choosing to go off-script actually caused the kidnappers to respond in such murderous fashion."

No one was safe from the spin. And soon, it would get worse....

RISE OF THE UNICORN

All before late afternoon.

Chapter 13

The bank customers were gathered up inside, blind and bound, close enough to a TV to hear the way the outside world was reacting to their situation. They all reflected in some way over Gus' interview, the one person out there whose name they knew was trying to help and the grim reality of their unfolding scenario. Meanwhile, Jones was fast running out of Unicorn teammates.

He retreated to the men's bathroom, entering while dispatching his masked disguise. The makeup was starting to run, and the mask had started choking him because of the steady heat both it and the situation generated.

Using his newly acquired expertise for make-up removal and no longer appearing to be white, he was returning to being Dr. Jones once more and looked himself over in the mirror. Just over his shoulder was his comrade, who secretly continued his work in that bathroom. Dr. Nolcox was the giant of a man who'd entered and never left the bathroom throughout this ordeal.

There were the two large plastic chemical barrels under the long, frosted windows which faced a row of tall hedges in the front of the bank. Each barrel had a wide tube that ran from its top and vented out an opening at the height of each window. The tubes had Velcro flaps built-in that were about six feet off the ground.

Dr. Jones handed off some items to his ally, who slipped them into the flaps and the barrels. This caused a chain reaction which sent fumes out and into the Southern California breeze that would dissipate any scent and carry the remaining particles whichever way the wind decided to blow – from one instant to the next.

His self-inspection complete, Jones turned, looked down to the floor and walked over. The hidden triage hosted one last patient on the air mattress to endure the last throes of encroaching sickness. He was ill and close to death, with a pallor over his dark skin.

"Know what?" Mr. Henry wheezed. "Fuck you."

Jones smirked.

"Fuck you right back, old man."

Mr. Henry fought off a grimace, then stifled a laugh.

"Helluva day," he said. "Just like you said."

Jones leaned against the nearby wall. "Couldn't pull it off without you."

"Damn right you couldn't," Mr. Henry said. "And I wouldn't've missed it for the world. This... this was an adventure right here."

An increase in the severity of his coughing called Jones to push off the wall to kneel next to the ailing man.

"So... you got everything in order?" Jones asked rhetorically.

"Oh yeah, oh yeah," he said with a sigh.

His breathing was becoming shallower, and his dimming eyes focused ahead on some spot beyond the ceiling.

"I tell you... unicorns were my daughter's idea?"

"You told me," Jones nodded. "Perfect name."

"Yeah," he replied. "Sure is."

He coughed a bit, but his body couldn't handle the full motion. The coughs got stuck halfway through, and he needed the next cough in line to push them up until all he could do was wheeze the rest out. He was still breathing. Just barely.

"Rational people don't believe in unicorns... but kids... kids do."

Jones reached down and took Mr. Henry's hand so he would know he wasn't alone. It felt, cold, and his skin felt like it was made from synthetic material.

"See, children ain't been scarred by the bullshit... of the world. They don't know that 'hurt people' hurt people. Unicorns is real... and they hide in plain sight..."

"Yes, sir," Jones agreed. "They sure do."

The next adventure beginning, Mr. Henry exhaled, smooth and clean. And then, just didn't inhale again. Jones fought back the tears and gritted his teeth.

"Mr. Henry?" he said. "Patrick...?" He checked the pulse on Mr. Henry's neck and gently released his hand.

"Gone?" Dr. Nolcox asked.

Jones sighed. "Not quite. But he's not coming back."

He again reached for his handgun and drew it out slowly. He tried to hold it in a tight, tense grip as if it were a fine and delicate tool, but this time his hand was shaking just a bit. This one... this one was always going to be hardest.

"Why don't I take care of that?" Nolcox asked.

Jones looked up at his partner. He already had his hands full, but his heart seemed much more open. Jones picked up the so-suave hat lying on the ground next to the soon-to-be-deceased. He dusted it off on his pants, blew on it for certainty and then laid it on a chest that was no longer rising and falling. After a moment, he gripped the pistol tight and handed it over carefully. He looked up at his partner. They exchanged a look of conflicting emotions, some degree of confidence but a renewed sense of certainty that what they were doing was the right thing to do. But the concrete finality in a mission like this, raises questions in even the strongest, and even when there is still much to accomplish.

"Are we gonna pull this off?" Jones asked.

"We better," Nolcox sighed. "Otherwise, what's the point? This was always bigger than us. Your plan? Brilliant. Given the cards we got dealt, I'm honored to be able to play a small part in this."

"Small?" Jones said. "Hardly."

Nolcox smiled awkwardly the way people who don't take compliments well, do before looking away briefly. When he looked back toward Jones, his eyes shone like he had a secret while he held the gun down at his side.

Knowing what that secret was, Jones nodded and then returned to the front interior of the bank while Nolcox went on with his work. He had to work a thin metal wire into a tiny set of spools that wrapped around the gears of a hand-made battery-powered pulley.

He turned to the near-dead old man, his only company, and watched as his final seconds on this plane ticked away...

...

Time was nearly up, and the importance of that time had been established with absolute certainty. Gus was back in his seat, and a pensive Shelly had never moved from her's. Fat Mike helped get them ready for a second time. He set the lavalier mic back into Gus' collar once again.

"We're cheering for you," he said, under his breath.

Gus nodded.

Fat Mike moved over to Shelly. She leaned her head back and flared her nostrils.

"Am I good?" she asked.

"Like a Vogue magazine cover," he replied, "Okay... in 15 seconds, people."

That was just barely enough time for Gus to check in on his televised companion. "Shelly -."

"I know," she said with a measure of defensiveness and humility. "Stick to the script."

"No," Gus said. "Trust your instincts. We're gonna get those folks outta there. You hear me?"

She looked at him, concerned.

He was resolute.

She nodded and turned to Fat Mike.

"Count us in, big man."

"In 5," he started, "4, 3, 2," and went silent on the last count before hand-signaling them in.

They were live.

RISE OF THE UNICORN

"I am Shelly Reyes here with Lieutenant Gus Martin, and we are coming to you live from what appears to be a, um, failed robbery attempt at Vista National Bank in the Toluca Lake community here in Los Angeles County. Before we, uh, stepped away, Lieutenant, you spoke about a hostage situation you navigated at a nail salon several months ago. Is there anything you'd like to add or clarify before I return to the list of questions given to me by The Unicorn?"

"Yes," Gus responded. "The loss of life that day...both the innocent victims in the shop and the two brave police officers... haunt me, even now. No loss of life is ever acceptable. But calculated, educated risks are a part of my job. Unfortunately, I was blamed for what occurred that day and subsequently used as a political tool by... well, a few members of the political machine. I was..." he began carefully because every word he spoke had an intention. "I was going through a difficult personal situation, but I was not distracted – in any way - during my job performance."

The speakers in the bushes came on. "Return to our questions," the warped voice demanded. "Begin with number 4."

Shelly turned her paper over to view it, as instructed. She could feel the weight of countless eyes; more people watching than at any other time in her career were on her and pressing judgment on her every action. They were on Gus too, but he remained eerily and utterly calm, a solid presence she could figuratively hold onto.

"Why do you believe The Unicorn are here?" she asked.

Gus nodded but gave no hesitation to his thought.

"The Unicorn... have a message they want to get a high level of visibility for. Something they feel is valuable enough to exchange for human life. I suspect we're getting to what that message is now."

"What is more valuable than money, Lieutenant Martin?" she asked. "And I want to clarify, quickly - his name is typed on this paper, which was handed to me in a sealed envelope from the captors just moments after we arrived on -."

"Because," Gus interrupted, "they specifically wanted me here, and they've manipulated this entire situation to accomplish it."

Gus turned to the camera, but he didn't see the millions of eyes watching over the situation as a matter of a thrilling media circus. He looked at the camera's lens as if he was looking directly at his target, his 'Arlene' because he was conducting a negotiation that happened to be separated by a couple of brick walls and numerous invisible airwaves.

"What do you want? Let's skip the games! What do you want!?"

The speakers again came alive and echoed before he and the steadily growing audience.

"We want our questions answered. What is more valuable than money, Lieutenant?"

"More valuable? Life. Life is more valuable than money. That's why we're here, right? To prove that life is more valuable than money."

A brief silence of consideration.

Then, the speakers activated once more, "Question number 7."

Shelly looked at Gus, concerned.

He nodded, "Ask it."

The people in the command center, the crowd out front and a growing national audience all stared at their devices and televisions in abject silence. Everyone wanted to know what was going to happen next.

Feeling that pressure, Shelly looked down at the paper to stabilize herself in order to read the question correctly and succinctly.

"What was the circumstance that caused you to be distracted? Provide a detailed answer, please."

"What?" Gus asked. "Is that what that says?"

He was incredulous, but that quickly turned into defiance.

"No." Gus shook his head. "No! Absolutely not!"

"I'm sorry?" she said.

Shelly's wordless voice raised with concern. And she braced herself to hear another round of shots from inside the bank.

"No," Gus insisted.

He turned from her to face the camera, pointing his finger at the lens – directly at the man inside the bank.

"That belongs to me, he - *you* don't get that!"

"You have 10 seconds to answer," the wireless speakers insisted.

"No deal," Gus folded his hands in his lap. "I want hostages. Give. Mc. Hostages!"

He sat and stared at *him*, unblinkingly stoic, as ten slow seconds passed. Everyone held their breath and braced together. Millions of people counted to ten at different rates. Far too many were too slow with the count in their minds because they all jumped when the two gunshots went off.

Shelly fought the urge to look toward Gus for reassurance during the interview she was conducting.

It was just as well because the shots only served to anger him, and they awakened an energy or a force that had been dormant for far too long.

Mere moments later, Douglas came out again, this time with an elderly black man in his arms and a metal walker looping awkwardly around his arm. He placed Mr. Henry's body down, with the walker behind his head like a grave marker, and then, like a lost child, he slowly walked toward the police line.

The cops were at attention. No dirty tricks were played yet, but there was no margin for error.

Douglas was silently weeping; tears streamed down his face, as he repeatedly pointed back at the bank he was wandering away from. The officers quickly rushed him into custody, but not before Gus got a good, long, close-up look at him onscreen, and then he remembered exactly who he was.

Then, with millions of eyes upon him, he turned straight to the camera, undaunted.

"Was that your big move? Is that supposed to frighten us? You killing an innocent, unarmed, black man? If that's your chess move, then 'check.' You're hurting your own message. You're doing what's always been done. Getting what you want off the backs of Black folks. You want me to take my pants down – here, on television? Then you give me some of those people right now!"

It was a standoff.

For a negotiator, reframing a suspect's actions or intentions publicly was, without question, a highly dangerous play. In the eyes of the public, what Gus had, wasn't worth a human life. It certainly wasn't worth the money. Not yet. The previous conversation hadn't lapsed from the ears of those listening in a way that might resonate. The first gauntlet now thrown - Gus stood firm. Ready to be seen as a steely, arrogant cop flying over the edge. All the invisible tightropes of trust he was balanced on could not be seen through smartphone screens. But the television audience watched a dynamic energy shift with their larger screens.

"You want me to get to it?" Gus challenged. "Then let's get to it! Hostages." he said directly before adjusting his tone. "I *said,* hostages!"

A moment passed.

Then, the front door opened.

Six hostages in blindfolds walked out, ushered on by an unseen gunman from just around the corner, out of the sight of snipers or scouts. Six more lives were saved, seemingly at the cost of losing another one.

The collective police force breathed a sigh of relief, as well as many of the observers, but Gus remained determined. He stared dead straight into the camera with an unabating intensity.

Everybody everywhere was now waiting on Gus' next words.

"Children," he said finally.

The film crew snapped to attention.

"Children are more valuable than money."

He turned to Shelly.

"Now, re-ask the question."

"What?"

Shelly was on alert, frightened by what she perceived as her earlier mistake, swept up in the drama, and now she'd lost her place in the very real event they were living through because everything was happening in front of an infinite number of watchful eyes.

With a clear purpose in his expression, Gus leaned over and grabbed the paper meant only for her eyes. He took the list of demanded questions, balled it up and threw it on the ground before slowly pressing it under his foot until the life it had before was now gone.

"Ask me what you think they need to know," he said.

Shelly gave him a panicked, uncertain look, and Gus nodded to silently encourage her to continue.

It was his show now. He felt it.

Everybody felt it.

Chapter 14

Shelly faced Gus, about ¼ profile from the camera, so that most of her right side was showing and straightened her back. The sound of applause from a distant crowd a block away was audible but not captured over their mics.

"What, if anything," she began with a stiff, journalistic tone, "was distracting you during the time of the nail shop robbery?"

Gus took a breath in and puffed out his chest to face her, the camera, The Unicorn, the remaining captives, and the public all at once.

"Divorce, custody hearings... and how the Family Court System allows emotional abuse to be inflicted upon children while everybody pretends to care."

He turned to the camera.

"You said truth and authenticity? Well, I'm here now."

"Um, can you elaborate -."

"My ex-wife," he hadn't listened to Shelly because, at this point, he already knew what she was going to say, "left me for a rich guy. Life happens. Whatever. The hard part was watching her play the victim while she... assassinated my character. Telling a series of wild, but extremely calculated lies to anybody who'd listen. She did it to distract and deflect from what she'd really done... and to hide who she really was... is."

Gus nodded to Fat Mike off-camera and eyed something just off-screen. Fat Mike broke a cardinal rule of news reporting and let himself be seen, just an arm, handing Gus a cup of water to sip from. Then Gus continued.

"We share a son, and she used the Court System in two states to create absolute chaos. Why? To alienate me from our child. She didn't care if it hurt her own kid in the process... and it did. It really did."

Shelly nodded her comprehension before deciding, of her own accord, to press forward.

"Divorces and custody battles are notoriously difficult. You say children are systemically allowed to be damaged. How so?"

Gus stared directly into the camera, pondering the next step.

Gus knew his stare had gripped everyone watching this broadcast - including his team in the command center just a couple dozen yards away in the same parking lot. He stared right into the eyes of the would-be terrorists inside the bank. They were waiting on his answer... but he was waiting on them.

Randall watched over Kennedy's shoulder.

"What the hell is he doing?" he finally asked.

She felt it before stating it.

"Taking control," Kennedy said.

"By throwing everything away?" Danson asked, surprising herself while continuing to absorb the power in Gus' stare.

Suddenly, a realization became astonishingly clear for Danson.

"No... He's going after the hostages. Oh, shit."

Her eyes wandered to the LAPD feed of the bank's front doors, and she realized she was fighting back her unexpected tears.

"Well, I'll be damned," Logan said, genuinely impressed. "Look!"

The command center team all turned to view the larger monitor.

Five more hostages were coming out.

Officers managed to cover the body of Mr. Henry and carried it, on a stretcher to deliver him to the triage tent in the rear while the newly released others were taken into custody and issued one by one into what was becoming a barracks for the traumatized.

The stretcher was carried down the side street, which was, unfortunately, within sight of a small part of the crowd.

Sheila arrived there just in time to see him go. She spotted the walker first and then the slight hint of the jazzy suit underneath the covers.

"No!" she exclaimed. "That's my - he's my -."

Bird came up behind her and held her back from saying more. She turned and looked up at him. He had tears in his eyes as well and encouraged her to let it out against his shoulder.

They were hardly private enough to share their moment of grief. They'd both lost their father, and the story would be too good to pass up. Parts of the crowd turned to them when they couldn't get pictures or videos of the unfolding, unwinding crisis at the bank. Finally, and with much effort, the police arrived to try and calm things down around the siblings, who knew far more than they would ever let on.

Meanwhile, the interview proceeded.

"How are the children hurt systemically?" Gus repeated, picking up with his own wants temporarily satisfied, "Family Court is an assembly line. Everybody goes through the motions, the more outlandish the lies, the more likely the success. Evidence doesn't matter. The Law itself falls through the cracks between systemic incompetence and, to be fair, a massive overload of cases; Kids are left unprotected by just about everybody who is supposed to be their advocate."

Shelly nodded, and she continued as soon as she had the air to speak.

"Lt. Martin, sir? I realize this is very personal, but what you're saying sounds more philosophical than factual. What examples can you give that support your claims?"

"What examples do I have? That's funny," he said without a trace of irony. "Okay... Family Court records are sealed, but you've got resources, right?"

He waited for her to nod in confirmation.

"Criminal and Civil cases are available to anybody. Get your people to verify this... I went through 13 different Court hearings in 18 months in two states. For the out-of-state cases, I couldn't afford to pay another attorney. So, I represented myself against false police reports she filed like; attempted kidnapping - because I visited our son's school

- to hug him; physical abuse, and sexual abuse. Sexual abuse... my own kid."

Shelly took everything in while Gus continued.

"There were hearings where she attempted to change the jurisdiction of the case and others because I was, and continue to be, denied my scheduled visitation and biweekly Skype calls. She hovers over the calls I do get to control what he discusses or monitor his answers to innocent questions about the things she *allows* him to discuss with me. This... foolishness only frustrates, frightens, or confuses him because the sad little power game she plays is based on the fears within her mind. Nothing real."

He took another sip of water.

"Repeatedly, I'm found not guilty or 'insufficient evidence' gets stamped on the papers, but there's never any restitution for the time we lose and no... no meaningful punishment is handed to the person actually causing the problems."

He continued, "In 18 months, our child - my son - lost nine and a half months of visitation with me, a parent who wants to be with him. Worse? I can't tell him why when we do spend time together, or else, I'm accused of 'besmirching' his mother. Have your people check. See if I'm lying."

"And you represented yourself in several of the cases?" She asked.

"Couldn't afford an attorney. But I wasn't going to quit. My 'why' is my kid. Hell, I caught one of her lawyers - Lisa Lewinsky - in a lie so big she panicked and withdrew from the case. I even prove that to the judge, but no punishment for her either. Know why I just said her name? Cause I kept the receipts."

"Must've been terribly frustrating."

"Frustrating? I've tried to help so many parents since then - moms and dads. It seems like the System is just designed to keep poor people poor. But the most frustrating thing is watching real damage happen to your own kid and being unable to stop it."

Then Gus said something that almost didn't seem real... and he'd lived it. "He was made available to me for eight minutes last Father's Day. Not the three-day weekend the Court said I could have. Eight minutes. Who wins with that?"

Solid truth had been spoken, and, in keeping with the silent agreement that had been negotiated, another eight hostages were released, blindfolded, and following one another on orders from the gunman still inside. They were walking hand-to-shoulder in a sort of conga line.

And in the middle of that line was none other than Dr. Jones.

Gus snapped out of his brief daydream when he heard Shelly reporting that "More hostages are now being released."

Inside the bank, Dr. Nolcox continued to watch from a covered position. He had an iPad loaded up with a recording software suite and several stored voice lines recorded from different times and lengths. Everything he needed to keep the plan in action until the end. He gave a quick, quiet prayer, "Our Father, who art in heaven, hallowed be thy name," in quiet desperation as he listened to the news on the conference room TV.

Gus continued, "I actually get why some parents just walk away. There are so many well-meaning people in the world who simply aren't allowed to be parents... and it turns us into...into -."

Nolcox turned on the mic and clicked the button for the fourth of the prerecorded audio packets. Dr. Jones' now halting voice came through the speakers, still altered by technology.

"-into Unicorns. Something children believe in for as long as they can. Until the world convinces them that Unicorns don't exist. But Unicorns are always among us, in plain sight."

There it was.

The final word of The Unicorn, their message, their purpose.

The crowd overheard it, in person and online. It began a slow wave of conversation, a mild rise in the acceptance of the terrorist manifesto.

People nearly cheered for what Dr. Jones' recorded voice said, as if the dead bodies were never a thing to get them there.

"Sounds just like what my babies went through," a woman said.

"Dude is preaching the gospel!" a man shouted with conviction.

A dazed Gus returned to the moment.

"Anyway, that's all I got. If I was lying, I'm sure other people would've been killed by now." He turned to the camera, "There's your truth and authenticity. Now... how about what I want? All of the people you're still holding - especially the children."

A moment later, he got his wish. The last of the hostages crossed the front door's threshold with Angela escorting the three children in a group. The kids looked downright happy. Janelle cradled Sparkle in her arms.

The crowd cheered, seeing them safe.

The police, the media - everyone breathed a long, heavy but freeing sigh of relief.

The fresh breeze of optimism blew over everyone except Gus. He turned back to the camera, which continued to roll on local audio and only picked up clapping that was mistakable as white noise.

"How do I know that everybody's been released?"

A few seconds later, an answer came over the speakers.

"Come... in and see...for yourselves."

The voice sounded far weaker than it had before. It was still altered, but tired breathing had been inserted into the recorded performance.

...

Dr. Nolcox was on the bathroom floor. He had the air mattress while an unconscious George, sans his now disintegrated light blue jumpsuit, laid sprawled out on the cold tiles by the sinks.

Nolcox was sweating and weak.

He felt his mind slipping close to an edge he couldn't see, but its significance and purpose was unmistakable. He forced his hands together and brought them up to pray.

"Holy Mary, mother of God...pray for us sinners, now..." while the invisible edge slowly came toward him.

Chapter 15

The interview was over.

The camera briefly stayed on for Shelly to make a closing statement, but the scene rapidly shifted from their control. All Shelly could do from that point forward was stand by and let the crew take what images they could. It was a police matter now, and the police had their own procedures. Hopefully, the main perpetrator, the leader still inside the bank, would either be coming out in cuffs or under a sheet.

Gus jumped up from the canvass chair and waved Logan over.

The police captain was already on the radio coordinating a plan of entry involving other available officers who weren't already tending to the counselor tent or engaged in controlling the crowd.

Commissioner Kennedy leaned back in her seat. Her role continued to seemingly be observational as the unified precincts handled things according to established best practices. She wouldn't interfere or undercut the authority of her direct reports. She leaned to Randall and gave him a subtle assignment.

"When this is done, set up an immediate press conference using the front of the bank as a back-drop."

He nodded.

Once Gus arrived, all officers were at attention. He nodded to Logan whose renewed and profound respect for Gus was right there on his face... if you knew where to look.

Gus saw it.

Logan knew he'd seen it.

That was enough. The cops who'd lost their lives at the nail shop had been under his command. A fuller understanding demanded both deference and respect. For some, actions are apologies.

"Let's move!" Logan called.

The group swarmed to size and moved around the bank's every available exterior. While the officers up front prepared to engage, Gus kept the situation stable and negotiable. His job still wasn't done. His role still had to be fulfilled until he was certain that everyone was getting exactly where they should – by the book. Any hostages and their surviving captors.

"Hey! Let's keep the hostages separate from one another!" he ordered. "I need 10 or 12 of you stationed back here. Do not break these rear doors unless there's a reason."

Kennedy subtly joined in for the issuance of further orders.

"I want that crowd under control."

"Yes, ma'am," Logan replied. He went to his radio. "Stevie Pete? Have your group maintain your position. The Commissioner wants to maintain a crowd safety imperative."

"Roger that, sir," Peters replied.

Four shots, rapid but aimed, from inside.

Two sets of two, same as before.

The cops near the front went into a defensive crouch and aimed their weapons at the doors and windows. Logan and Gus pushed through to the front opening under cover. No further shots were heard.

It was either two hostages, taken as a power play before the police could ensnare them, or something else.

"Get the doors!" Logan commanded.

The officers moved forward. A pair tested the doors. They were unlocked, and through the glass, they saw no defenses. Logan continued.

"Martin and I are going in. I want a six-man point up front, fingers off until you hear a shot, seek cover, and make a defensive advance. Ready?"

"Ready!"

"Ready... Move!"

At Logan's command, the team rushed in. Six men in body armor wielding shotguns broke through first and secured the walk-in lobby, then they moved forward and secured positions behind cubicles away from the open main lobby space. Gus and Logan stayed near the back and assessed the situation between short-form codes to move and hold positions.

The lights were on, and the TVs in the corner were still broadcasting the scene of the bank itself from the outside. Aside from a few cut phone cords, the bank was untouched as far as they could tell. No chaos, blood stains, tears in the carpet, or holes in the walls.

A neat and tidy crime scene with nobody in sight.

"Securing evidence," an officer said.

There were some cut-up zip-ties, an uneaten mashed sandwich, and other inoffensive debris on the floor, mostly made by the hostages. Nothing dangerous or essential. The officers continued to move in a widespread which covered a full range of the lobby and personal banking areas.

Logan and Gus kept to the middle. A systematic intrusion.

Then, suddenly, there was a scraping sound coming from the bathrooms. It was the men's bathroom near the front door. The officers used hand signs and guided one another to the entrance with Logan at the back. Two were ready to charge in, two to cover them from behind, and another two held back behind the nearest counter.

Gus put his hand up to keep them all back. Logan nodded and let Gus walk forward. The officers at the wall stepped to the side; one made some extra room on the wall for Gus to press against.

"LAPD!" Gus called. "You are surrounded. Drop to your knees, lock your hands behind your heads and announce that you are cooperating with my commands."

No response. Not in words.

The scraping continued. It sounded like... metal on tile, with occasional bumps in the rhythm where an angled surface hit the grades between the tiles. Then, something bumping around like it came from inside a container.

Gus tried again.

"Keep your hands where we can see them! Tell me you understand!" No response.

He nodded to the man across the door from him.

"We are now entering the room!"

The officer pushed the door open, and Gus slipped over to his side. Not enough to catch a glimpse of anything significant before the door swung shut. Logan took over Gus' spot on the wall and held it open on the next push. The two officers entered first, followed by Gus.

At that moment, Gus had to take in the entire scene and decide, based on what he saw, with what his brain could process to be the next course of action.

First, two bodies on the ground.

Shots to the heart, blood oozing. Then the dragging noises. He looked over and saw the two plastic barrels by the window, opaque white but too thick to show just how much fluid was in them. The low whirring noise they hadn't heard until they were in the room was a mechanism inside the long funnel tubes that led into the barrels sealed with Velcro. Already inside one of the tubes was an iPad and two mechanized racks with pullies, but outside the other were the two guns that had been dragging across the tile floor. Both were now being pulled up along a thin wire about to enter the tube's Velcro flap opening.

"Keep the guns from going in the -." Gus' order came too late.

As if, at his signal, the objects were dropped.

The plastic barrels sloshed with a muffled fizzling sound.

The small traces of fumes present in the air informed the well-trained officers that they were dealing with a potent hydrofluoric acid that had worked overtime, dissolving more than the odd piece of clothing on the floor. Any physical evidence that had existed was likely gone forever.

The Unicorn had proved themselves to be professionals in the highest sense. They'd made their point, delivered their message, and left nothing behind but that message....

A few moments later, Commissioner Kennedy entered under the escort of the rest of the team as the police began their broader sweep of the bank interior. She looked at the established scene and stood over the two deceased on the floor, dead of an elaborate suicide. She looked up and saw two hooks screwed into the plaster ceiling where the guns must have hung, which then slipped out as the mechanism dragged them into the acid. She couldn't help but suck her teeth while appreciating the ingenuity and the grandeur that had placed both men here to make their transitions over to the hereafter.

"So... this is the mastermind behind this whole thing. The Unicorn ringmaster."

She looked at Nolcox first, then George. The bodies didn't bother her. What they'd done while alive did. She turned to Logan.

"Get forensics in here so we can reverse engineer this."

"Geez," Logan said. "This son-of-a-bitch is one big dude. Okay, let's clear out and double-check the rest of the interior."

Gus was on his way out but walked over to look down at the two bodies again. First George's body then that of Dr. Nolcox.

His mind began to race, playing everything back at an ever-increasing speed, and then, he felt his heart scream. It was loud in his mind, but it all resulted in a simple whisper as the dreadful statement quietly escaped his lips.

"That's not him."

He turned and raised his voice. "Commissioner Kennedy!"

"Over here," she said, moving out of the bank's front doors.

The whole bank scene was buzzing with police already.

Gus followed her out as she strode to the rear to prepare for her statement to the press.

"Walk with me."

"Commissioner!" Gus whispered. He kept his voice soft, afraid of the information he now carried. "Commissioner!"

"What?" she asked. "You're gonna get your gold star, Lieutenant. Helluva job under the circumstances. Helluva job—"

"That's not him," he said. "That's not the guy."

She scrunched her face at his suggestion like he'd slipped a lemon into her mouth.

"What do you mean that's not the guy?"

"That's not who I was talking to - who I was dealing with."

"You've been under a ton of pressure. I get that -."

"It's not him!"

She stopped, saw that he was serious, and with palpable irritation, pulled out a photo from her coat pocket. It was part of the assembled bundle of evidence and images taken from his earlier hidden-in-plain-sight phone camera trick. It was of the leader standing in front of the bank's back door. In front of the color-coded height indicator.

"Look. This still is from the video you recorded. White man, gray hair, damn near 7 feet tall—"

"What?" Gus said. "No, he wasn't that tall."

"Okay," Kennedy said, clearly agitated. "Six-seven or six-eight. Whatever. We just saw him – his body - in person. He's that tall. Look at the picture! The height measurements are right behind where he's standing. This is the guy."

Gus stopped, shocked. He couldn't believe it.

He had an image of the scene in the bank captured perfectly in his mind, better than what the camera picked up, and the man in the bathroom did not match the specifics of the man who he'd been dealing with.

Kennedy continued onward while Gus remained until he felt another path calling.

He needed to check what he knew to be true before Forensics got too far into their work. He needed to make sure that the man he'd been talking to did not somehow slip away.

After all, if the victims killed were all part of the same outfit, some of those hostages could have been working with them as well.

Was Douglas just a distraction to show it was possible to confuse or pollute Gus' mind?

Was the game still on?!?

Chapter 16

Gus decided to circle back to follow up with his instincts. He re-entered through the front door to check what he remembered against what he could see in the present. Standing where he was when he'd come in to get a read on the condition of the hostages, Inspector Wiley meandered up from just behind him.

"Hey. Great job, Martin!" the old, gray-haired Columbo look-alike said. "Geez, I can't imagine doing what you did back there. You know? Some of that stuff you were talking about. The same shit happened to me! It was a hundred years ago, but wow... My kids hate my guts to this day. But what are you gonna do, right? Helluva thing. But you fucking called it!"

"Thanks, Wiley," Gus said mechanically. He turned back around, stepped further into the bank lobby, and gave it a look around. He stood much further in than he had when the crisis was happening in real-time. The man was certainly taller than Gus, but not by such a ridiculous degree. And certainly not close to seven feet tall. Was he? The deceased older man he'd just seen on the bathroom floor was too long for their blankets to cover. That couldn't be the same guy.

"Hey, big shot," Wiley called out. "Now, don't go fucking up my crime scene there."

Gus wasn't listening. He already had what he needed, a long, full view of the place from where he'd initially stood. Now he was heading over to where the group's leader had been standing.

The guns were in the acid, as was the iPad with the unfiltered audio. Melted. Still, Gus was outpacing the inspector at determining just how much was planned and how much everybody was missing. How much the Commissioner herself was missing.

Standing at the back doors looking all the way over to the front, where he'd been standing, was weird. Was the leader of The Unicorn so arrogantly conniving as to believe he could fool an entire police department? His eyes scanned the area before slowly turning around. Then, he looked to his left and found his answer was right there on the wall.

"Oh, you motherfucker," Gus muttered.

There was no color-coded height indicator on the wall, not glued, etched, or painted. Just the slightest presence of residue from some painter's tape that let him know that one had been there.

Chances were good; the tape and the height indicator chart had already dissolved in the bottom of a barrel. Along with any clothing or uniforms the masterminds had worn or exchanged when it was time to walk out with the hostages or die for the cause.

Gus left in a stilted hurry to review the evidence they had gathered in the command tent, all the way up until well past the dinner hour. Then he was ushered with the rest of the officers to the press conference at the makeshift podium in front of the bank where Commissioner Kennedy wrapped the whole thing up.

He was there but entirely unfocused. Anyone who saw him didn't expect a sterling report from the embattled negotiator who had just opened his entire personal life to a global viewing audience. But he, undoubtably, looked significantly absent from the scene.

Meanwhile, Commissioner Kennedy continued her speech about what the police did as if she had been the one commanding it all.

But that's the way the game is played, he reasoned.

"... and although there were several unfortunate casualties, I think we would all agree that Lieutenant Augustus Martin - one of the department's top negotiators - did a tremendous job under quite abnormal circumstances. As I mentioned, we are still in the process of identifying some of the deceased and, of course, notifying the next of kin, so we will not be naming names at this juncture, and I would appreciate the Media's cooperation in honoring our position. Obviously, I can't take any questions at this time, but we will keep you informed as we learn more."

Bulbs went off at Commissioner Kennedy, the numerous police officers and Gus, who she signaled to step up and join her. He said nothing, looked as stern as ever and continued to deepen his thinking. That night was the start of the first of many rounds of interrogations with the hostages.

Gus made his assertion clear that the victims - the dead ones - were somehow in on the failed heist, to the higher-ups. They had been sacrificed and used as a showy distraction the ringleader created for the public, but all of the real hostages were freed. It sounded far-fetched when he heard himself say it, and he saw the looks on the faces of the few people he reported to, but he'd connect the dots for them later. He'd make them understand.

First, the interrogations needed to occur.

For the hostages-turned witnesses, it was simple deductive questioning to help close the case from a police reporting perspective. The job of interviews was split between Gus and Logan. Captain Powell even came in off-duty to help lessen the workload and get to the bottom of things while Randall watched everything on the monitors as he'd been instructed. But the rooms where they conducted their sit-downs were still called interrogation rooms. Gus had a list of requested subjects to talk to, the ones who were the most involved at the bank and were there the longest, as well as the ones who, for some reason, willingly stepped forward to help the most.

"Douglas Weimar," Gus began.

He looked across the table at the big man. He was much calmer and together than when they'd first met. He'd had time for the situation to settle in his mind and time with his kids to assess and assure their safety and well-being. He was former military, so he'd been able to compartmentalize his assigned duties for 'body removal.' That part made sense.

Initially, he seemed guarded and answered Gus with quiet nods and monosyllabic responses.

"Okay, Douglas, once again, I am Lieutenant Gus Martin - you can call me Gus - and this is just a quick meeting where you can help me by answering some questions."

"Okay," Douglas said.

"And if you don't understand a question, you can say that. If you don't know the answer, you can say that. Just be honest, truthful with your responses, and stick to the questions as I ask them."

"Got it."

"All right. Now, you were going to the bank that day from your home, correct?"

"Yes."

"And you went inside with your two kids - they're Chris and -."

"Zoey, yes."

"Okay. Why did you pick that day to go to the bank?"

Gus looked up. He could see a troubled look in Douglas' eyes. Like he was confused. Douglas was the one handling the bodies at the door. He was high up on a list of potential suspects left alive by the ringleader.

Gus wanted to clear him, but only if he could.

"Just a normal day," he answered. "I, uh...I'd thought of doing it that day because it was one of the few times that week, I knew I'd have both kids to myself. Not that - not that the wife and I are having problems. Um..."

He stammered to himself quietly and evaded Gus' eyes. He'd touched on a subject the whole world now knew about and associated with Gus at that point. Gus simply nodded for him to continue.

"Chris has soccer practice, and Zoey's been playing with her friends more lately. Annie - that's my wife, Anna - well, she gets so tired after work most days she can't even cook. It's that way mostly in the spring because of her allergies... so I wanted to take the kids out to eat for breakfast, and I had to go by the bank. So, I brought them with me."

"What did you have to go to the bank to do?"

"Just a quick withdrawal," he explained. "I pay a few of our home utilities in cash for on-site work. I like to give them some, you know, under-table money. It's nothing illegal. It's just - checks and automatic payments can bounce, and I've been there. I've been in a place where I needed money, and the bank's online service gave me the runaround with it. But cash is just cash, you hand it over, and they can use it that day. It's easier."

"But you can use your debit card at the restaurant. Right?" Gus asked.

"Yeah... but the more places you use, it makes it easier to steal your card info."

Gus ignored that and moved on.

"Okay. Did you see the main guy who took the bank hostage?"

Douglas nodded. "Yes."

"Can you describe him?"

"Uh, tall. Tall man, wearing a long coat. Deep voice. He - I don't want to do any sort of typecasting or anything like that. But he was talking about infidels and stuff, but he wasn't...he didn't look like someone, you know, like that."

"Not Middle Eastern?"

"No - and no, and I wouldn't assume that. But you know how people - they wave a flag or have an anarchy shirt on nowadays, the ones who make those kinds of declarations. This guy wasn't screwing around, but he just looked like a... guy. Who went out with a raincoat on."

Gus took out a photo from his file. Of one Dr. Lorenzo Nolcox, taken from a hospital staff website listing, as well as photos of the same man, post-death, taken by crime scene photographers.

"Mr. Weimar, I have these photos. Does the man in them look familiar?"

Douglas looked at the photos carefully. He processed them between the slightly smiling professional with a thick gray mustache above and the very similar, but sunken-eyed and the placid-faced man below.

"Is this him?" Gus asked. "The man who held you captive?"

"I think so," Douglas said. "Yes."

He didn't sound sure. Gus took the pictures away and slid them into his folder.

"Mr. Weimar, do you visit that bank frequently?"

"Not too frequently. Once a week at most unless something comes up."

"On the wall," Gus began, "in the rear entrance - the one you used, in fact - do you recall a height chart on the wall near the door there, on the backside of the lobby?"

Douglas stared into the distance to try and resurface a memory of such an insignificant detail, while his mind raced with further inquiries as to why he had to know. He went over his inner file of times when he'd stopped by or noticed a height chart. It took him a few seconds to get out an answer.

"I'm not sure."

"That's all right," Gus assured him.

The confusion and uncertainty were something he was looking for.

"Did you speak to your son and daughter about the experience?"

Douglas sighed. "Yes."

"Did you explain...the role that you took?"

"...I told them that the bad men – people - wanted me to do something, and I did it so no one else would get hurt."

The "people" correction meant "not all men" which confirmed other elements Gus knew about that Douglas likely didn't. The two men stared at one another until Gus decided he'd seen and heard enough.

"Okay...Mr. Weimar, we'll be in touch with you to wrap this all up. You go home to your kids and hold them tight."

"Y-yes. Thank you." He said.

Douglas left, feeling one step closer to freedom. It was evident to Gus that Douglas was just in the wrong place like everyone else there. He was searched thoroughly for bombs and any other foreign objects when he exited the bank, including money. No notes, no writing, nothing could indicate that something was in it for him. And no external motivation in his personal life. A dead end. Good for Douglas, and not so bad for Gus.

He'd just narrowed down the list of potential suspects by one more...

Chapter 17

The interrogations continued through the night.

Gus met and talked to a few of the civilians who were involved, and most of them either broke down in tears or cursed out their captors from this side of the veil.

Two days later, things began again with a better grasp on the situation. All the accounted-for hostages recovered from the bank that day were kept on a close retainer and forced to stay in their homes and not travel until a time came when they could clearly be released from any suspicion. Douglas was close. He had an exit interview with Logan to go over his mental state, but that was it. Gus' day had a few key meetings he had to work through, so he set up the room as best he could.

"Dr. Winston Jones?" he called.

Dr. Jones entered the room.

Everything about him was professional. He'd cleaned up since the incident but still looked a bit haggard like he'd lost some good sleep. Gus went over his notes on the good doctor and turned to his whiteboard. He arranged many necessary pictures of the deceased, all taken when they were alive, and had them strung up with magnets. Dr. Jones quickly looked at the whiteboard before he sat and turned to his interrogator.

"Hello, sir," Jones began.

"Hello again, doctor," Gus started. "Thank you for coming."

"Of course. Anything to get this ordeal behind us."

"Yes. So, I'm going to ask you a few questions about what happened, and I need you to answer to the fullest of your ability. If there's a question you don't understand or a detail you don't recall, just let me know, and we can move on."

"Certainly," Jones said.

"Great. Now then, on that day - we're referring to the day of the robbery - you were present?"

"Yes."

"At around what time did you enter the bank?"

"Um, around 9:20, maybe. I don't know exactly when."

"Okay. What particular reason made you choose to go to the bank that day."

"I have several clients - private therapy sessions up in the hills and the like - who pay in cash or checks. I came in from a meeting with a client who had requested me earlier that morning for somewhat of an emergency. Anyway, I wanted to deposit their money. Cash."

"Okay," Gus said.

"Anything beyond that would stray into doctor-patient -." Jones said.

"That's fine. You answered my question. Anything more than that can go through legitimate legal channels. I'm not forcing anything out of you." Gus said.

Dr. Jones lifted his hand apologetically.

Gus continued. "Now, when the robbery began, where were you?"

"In the bathroom," Jones replied.

"Were you aware of what was happening outside?" Gus asked.

He shook his head. "I heard gunshots and - and I just sat down and hoped they wouldn't come find me," Jones replied.

"Did they?" Gus asked.

"Yes. A man -." He looked to the whiteboard and to the picture of George, which he pointed at. "Him. Row two, four across. He found me and pointed a gun at my face. Ordered me to walk with him out to the lobby area."

"How long, in your best guess, would you say it took between the first gunshots going off and you being kidnapped?" Gus asked.

"A minute, if that," Jones said.

"And it was that guy up there?" Gus asked.

"Yes. His picture on your board is - I didn't see him smile. He was more furious and demanding."

"What did he tell you to do?" Gus asked.

"Stand up, move, eyes on the floor. He led me from behind with the gun at my back." Jones replied.

"Okay. Now - do you frequent this bank?" Gus asked.

"Fairly regularly. I go there when I'm in the area or on my way to my home which is only a few miles away." Jones replied.

"Do you know the layout of this particular bank fairly well?" Gus asked.

"Somewhat," Jones replied.

"When you were being escorted, were you able to tell what room you were being taken into?" Gus asked.

"Yes, a conference room. On the, uh, sit-down banking side." Jones replied.

"Personal banking. And that's where you stayed for the duration of the situation?" Gus asked.

"As soon as I got in, they tied my hands behind my back and blindfolded me. The same thing they did to everyone else inside."

"They were already blindfolded?" Gus asked.

"I, uh... I guess most were." Jones replied.

"I see," Gus said.

Gus jotted some notes down from what they went over. Jones looked over at the whiteboard again. His eyes passed over some of the pictures with a lost fondness. He asserted a more firm, stoic brow when Gus looked back at him.

"I want to walk you through one by one if you recognize any of the people on that board, aside from the man you mentioned already. Did you get a good look at the man in charge?"

"No," Jones said. "I followed instructions to keep my eyes down. I did hear another man speaking and giving instructions but never saw him."

"Okay. And you were in the conference room - who else was in there?" Gus asked.

"I don't know. I mean... I do see some of them on your board there." Jones said.

"Okay. When they were broadcasting the interview that I - um, how did the people... where you were listen to it?" Gus asked.

"There is a television in there. I think they played it from that." Jones said.

"Okay," Gus said.

"And that was you speaking, Lieutenant?" Jones said.

"Yes, it was," Gus said.

Jones gave a sympathetic nod.

"Were any of your personal belongings taken from you?" Gus asked.

Jones sighed. "I carry a small pocketknife, partly for protection. It honestly did not occur to me to use it. They took it from me when they tied me up. But nothing else."

"I see. Mr. Jones, how did you arrive at the bank that day?"

Dr. Jones had a curious look on his face. "I drove."

"You drove yourself?" Gus asked.

"Yes. Despite being a psychiatrist to the stars, I do enjoy a nice drive now and then."

"Okay."

Gus wrote something else down.

"You were captured by that guy, and you are aware of one other person involved. Did you see anyone else participating in the robbery - or hear after you were blindfolded - other than them?"

"I'm sure there had to be more, but I can't give a guess as to how many. At least two, I would say. One was a woman. Her." Jones said.

He pointed to Lisa in a picture taken before her death.

"Okay..." Gus said.

Their interview dwindled into some double-checking of personal details to help round off any external suspicions, and Gus led him back out.

His next interview was with Angela, the personal banker who seemed to suffer the most emotional injury from the incident. She sat down and was already taking long, dragging breaths to keep herself from sobbing.

"Hello, Ms. Gutierrez," Gus greeted.

"Hello, Lieutenant," she replied.

Her tone was consistently thankful, very measured, and polite but also almost constantly fighting back the tears.

"I'm going to ask you a few questions about the day of the robbery, what you remember, what you recall. If you don't know or can't quite remember you can just tell me what you do know." Gus said.

"All right. I'll try. It's all - it's all still in there, but when I think about it, it's like - I feel like I'm getting sent back to relive it." She said.

"Just relax," he said. "You're deep in the police station. The safest place you can possibly be. Just focus and reply to me when I ask you something, all right?"

"Mm," she nodded. She was already gulping to fight back the tears.

"How long have you been working at Vista?" Gus asked.

"Four years," Angela replied.

"Full time?" Gus asked.

"Part-time to start. I got - I was a trainee teller for the first few months, but they bumped me up because Margaret - the senior teller who trained me- left, and they needed a spot to fill. I mean, a person to fill the spot. But - but I also have a finance degree, so I could. Now, I mostly tend to personal accounts during the day, but I'll help on the teller side when they are short on staff, you know. Keep things moving." Angela replied.

"Okay - thank you. You answered my question at the start there. That's all I'm looking for." Gus said.

She sighed and nodded, just barely holding herself together.

"Now," Gus continued, "where were you on the floor when the robbery began?"

"I was in my office," she said, "my cubicle. It's the first on the right if you're facing that side from the tellers, midway to the front entrance. I was helping Mr. Henry," she paused, "a client, who wanted to take care of some things."

Gus looked over at his wall of faces and pointed to the sly-looking older black man wearing a hat at a rakish angle. "Him?"

"Yes," she said, barely looking. "He's a regular. He was operating on a fixed income and needed to readjust his spending from time to time, and I was trusted with his account. He made extra money sometimes and was making plans for, uh..."

She fully stopped and tried to control her breathing.

"Easy, Ms. Gutierrez. Breathe and stay calm." Gus said. She took a few calming breaths and nodded.

"Sorry," Angela replied.

"It's fine. Totally understandable. Now then..."

Gus continued walking on eggshells with Angela through the proceedings of the event. It all played out similar to the accounts given by other customers who were in the bank that day, but Gus was quick to note certain exceptions toward the end of her recollection.

"Where were you before being released?"

"Oh, they picked me up and took me somewhere - the break room, I think. And then they - he - the guy, whoever he was, he took out a knife, and I was so scared. He cut off my ties, led me to Cathy's office where the kids were, and told me I had to watch out for them until everything was over. It was then, at that point, I knew he – they weren't going to kill us. That something else was going on but that we were going to be okay, you know?"

Gus saw that she was reliving everything as she continued. "He came to check on us once or twice more, but only by cracking open the door and talking to us. We never saw him anymore. Then, in the end, it was another man – another voice – who came to tell us it was time to go. He just made sure we looked at the floor until we got to the front doors and came outside. By then, everyone was already gone, and I didn't look back. I couldn't. I did what the first guy said - led the kids out like I was told, and then, that was it."

"So, you were in the conference room," Gus clarified, "until they pulled you away from there and took you into the employee break room?"

"Yes. They took Mr. Henry... and me." She said.

He sidestepped the reference so she wouldn't become emotional again.

"You were blindfolded that whole time," Gus asked.

"Pretty much... Yes, I was." She said.

"Were you aware of anyone else in the break room with you?" Gus asked.

"No. I heard them - the robbers talking, occasionally, about the plan going well. And they were, like, supporting each other to keep going or whatever. Maybe some of them were put up to it or they didn't want to do it. I think they might have been good people but somehow got forced into all of this and - and -."

"It's okay, Ms. Gutierrez, no pressure. Nice and easy." Gus said.

Angela was almost out of energy just from beating back her sobbing. She nodded and tried not to cry. Gus motioned over to the board. On one side were the suspects counted as dead, and on the other were bank employees and the customers that were hostages, but for the purpose of the interviewees, Gus did not mark which side was which. "Do any of these people look familiar?"

"Yes," she said.

"Your co-workers?" Gus asked.

"Yes." She said.

"And who else?" Gus asked.

"Uh - Mr. Henry," she pointed out, "and Mr. Jones – Dr. Jones. And I think - wait! Him!" She pointed at Miguel. "And her - they were in on it! They were wearing blue jumpsuits that day. They were part of the group working on the renovation or whatever, but when the shots went off, they pulled out guns and were part of it!"

Gus wrote something down. A confirmation of an existing report he'd already read, but it helped calm her building feelings.

"Did they work there regularly?" Gus asked.

"No, they just - they started a few days before. I was on opening duty to help unlock things and get set up, and they were waiting outside. They'd worked some the day before, fixing things around the interior and doing stuff outside. I - I let them in because they were Cathy's people – Cathy O'Brien..."

She again collected herself before continuing.

"Cathy was the one who'd taken the bids for the job and who made the recommendation to upper management. Anyway, I let them -." She said.

"You let them in?" Gus asked.

"And I - I let them in. I was - I -."

She broke down. Gus got up and tried to comfort her with a hand on her shoulder.

"It's okay. Take your time. Try to recall all the people you remember from that day, and we'll arrange them on this board. Employees, customers and the... the workers."

She nodded glumly. It didn't take very long, and there were many who she never selected for any category. A short time later, Gus helped her up and walked her out. Of course, she had to come back, but her duty was already over for the day. And she gave him plenty of information to work from... even through the tears.

Slowly, the case was coming together. The game was just about up...

Chapter 18

Justice moves slowly. Gus knew that. The people he negotiated with often knew that, but those seeking it rarely remembered.

Even he was guilty from time-to-time... of knowing the System as it worked for and against him. But he finally made progress. His board had more clutter than before, links with lines and post-it notes connecting people in unexpected ways.

The suspects all managed to line up based on the testimonies, and he made even more connections through his laptop. He was downright investigating the case, forward and back. One of the interrogation rooms was converted into his own temporary office as he collected data from the web and offline.

He picked up his phone and mutely dialed a number. Bags were set under his eyes. He was one coffee too many in a caffeine-driven fervor. He was getting too close to giving up, too close to giving in. The line connected.

"Hello, can I speak to -. Yes, I know. I apologize for calling at this hour. I just wanted to - ensure we're being thorough in our follow-up investigation. In memory of those who, like your uncle who, um, lost their—Hello? Hello?"

They hung up. Not a good answer, but not nothing. He didn't even need them to talk. He already got what he needed from their rejection and their social media pages. Gus sat back from his computer screen and blinked his tired eyes.

He grabbed a remote and switched on the TV. It was usually for showing closed circuit recordings to suspects and interviewees to help jog their memories of what they'd done or maybe what they should have seen, but, from time to time, it also functioned as a way to see beyond the concrete walls and out into the rest of the world. This time the governor of California appeared on-screen, and it looked like he was at the tail-end of an early-morning press junket. One of many in a series from the fallout of the crisis with The Unicorn a few days prior.

"I've received a ton of phone calls and emails from our California constituency who are expressing their very valid concerns regarding how the state's Family Courts handle caseloads and the emotional impact that some children experience, as a result of, uh... parental or situational conflict. So, of course, we need to form a committee in order to take a hard look at how things are handled presently and..."

Gus leaned out of his seat, stood up and began pacing around in front of his whiteboard of connections while the newest political football game played out on the airwaves.

He'd done a ton of leg work, but somehow... it felt like the race was fixed. Everyone was already satisfied with the present conclusion except for him. The main concern seemed to move on to local extremist terror prevention, which was even criticized over the recent *capitulation* to the extremist rhetoric from higher circles of influence. That The Unicorn were never supposed to exist, and that attention should not be granted to a random bank robbery or the 'celebrity officer' who helped put a stop to it.

Blah-blah-blah-blah.

Gus tried to continue working, but the 'ding' announcing the arrival of an urgent email changed all of that. He thought it was another communique - or perhaps, another hair-brained threat - but it was something slightly more ominous.

This email had come straight from Commissioner Evelyn Kennedy's office, and it was worded like it came from the guy... that assistant of her's... Randall. Gus only skimmed it enough to make his brow furrow before he would hurriedly exit his makeshift office to attend an immediate meeting.

Upon his arrival, it was clear the real conversation had already taken place between City officials who hadn't deemed him worthy of their presence. This part was quite perfunctory, and it wasn't really a conversation. It was a formality - where neither his participation nor his opinion was required. He was being told how things were going to go. Period. It was done nicely – all things considered. But the message was crisp and clear – although his response remained unchanged.

"It just feels like," Gus said, "I'm being thrown under the bus here. In fact, that's exactly what's going on."

Commissioner Evelyn Kennedy sat behind her desk, arms folded atop it like a lioness, and gave him a look of no quarter.

"Lieutenant? I have already explained that there are a lot of moving parts to this situation. You being named in several lawsuits against the LAPD for some of the lives we lost at the bank a few nights ago... require me to take actions you may not fully grasp right now. You are not being fired. You are not being thrown under the bus. This is a paid administrative leave. Essentially a vacation - with the singular condition that you abide by–"

"A gag order," he said.

She nodded, understandingly, at his frustration.

"A gag order of sorts, Gus. I need you to leave this incident's families and the survivors alone. You don't believe we're hanging this on the right guy, and I'm telling you, for reasons bigger than both of us, it needs to be him. Now, are we clear?"

Gus stared at her with frustration and conviction – which could've been interpreted as insolence, yet was allowed or, perhaps, ignored.

"Lieutenant? Do you remember the manner in which you asked me to put my trust in you that day? I do. You pulled the hotep, brotha/sista card, which I clearly heard but chose to ignore. But I made my decision because I trusted and believed in you. You, your capabilities, and your expertise. Your very unprofessional 'effects of slavery' reference was not a factor... but here, now... my denying its accuracy wouldn't be being honest."

She saw they were going nowhere, so she changed direction and softened her tone to emphasize her personal, empathetic point.

"I am looking at the larger picture here, and I see things coming your way that you cannot - at least not right now. Gus, I'm telling you... your life is going to change in ways you cannot even fathom. So, as equally unprofessional as this may be, I am asking you, and I am ordering you... to place your trust in me – because 'we,'" she emphasized, "need to trust each other. Allow me to do what I do."

Gus met her gaze and felt the intensity and sincerity in it.

He understood whose side she was on, which was a tricky question one word or phrase couldn't adequately cover. So, resigned to the reality of what was, Gus simply nodded his 'yes' and accepted his position. His fate.

It was beyond him. Not for justice, but for optics and politics. All of the things the rest of the team needed to keep going to cover their butts or do the work they felt needed to be done. So, because there really was no option, Gus acquiesced.

In the span of a few minutes, the case he'd come in the door with no longer existed except within his mind.

And that is exactly where the case was left to fester – in his mind and his gut. Despite his acceptance, being on administrative leave, allowed him the freedom to continue working on the case that no longer existed from the privacy of his home.

Numb to the performative aspects of his situation, Gus was okay with being celebrated by some and maligned by others.

He was clear on the 'what' and 'why' his being shuffled out of the light while the case was reframed, reimagined, and then cleanly, quietly wrapped up, gnawed at his spirit. But he decided not to allow himself to fall into yet another dark hole because of decisions made concerning him by those simply in the position to do so. He'd had enough of dark holes. He knew exactly who he was, and their little decisions regarding his case may serve their purposes, but he defined himself by himself and grew even more potent as a result.

Everyone involved that day was ready to move on from the harrowing and deadly incident. Quickly.

Both established and new bank customers returned or arrived at the revamped Vista National facility with new, tighter security measures in place.

Some employees from that day understandably took time off to reassess their lives and emotionally recover, and most came back one after another to resume job roles, and some took on new ones.

Angela had been promoted to Branch Manager-in-training until she could officially take the late Cathy O'Brien's formal position through internal accreditation and training coursework.

Douglas and his kids thoroughly removed themselves from public discourse and lived privately.

Patricia maintained a civil suit against the major shareholder group that owned the bank for emotional compensation, which seemed to be going well.

The video surveillance arm of Vista National, which was broken into, took its own emergency measures to repair the degrading situation as they were involved in the robbers taking power, and the perpetrators were being tracked by specialists who, according to news reports, were supposedly close to closing in. But nothing ever came of it, of course.

Two months passed, and in all that time, not a single soul came wandering around to Dr. Jones to ask what he thought or felt about all the fallout from the incident.

At least, not until he opened his door to the familiar sight of the famed, Black, formerly embattled negotiator from the LAPD...

Chapter 19

Two months out of the daily grind made Gus feel like a new man. He was refreshed, and even better, he was in the clear.

The LAPD absorbed most of the suits and whittled them down to mere degradations and impunity. Nothing stuck or lasted as the evidence continued to mount putting the deceased under a different interpretation. Everything stayed quiet, but Gus remained on administrative leave and did his work without hurting any more feelings. And all that work led him to one of the 43 mansions surrounding Toluca Lake.

The home of Dr. Winston Jones.

Strolling up the sleek walkway, Gus passed the car in the driveway, a classic Porsche 911, sleek and silvery, with accented headlights and a steeper back, like something out of a Bond film.

"Sweet ride," he said to himself.

His own car, a brand-new red Mustang, didn't disappoint, though.

The two men had different styles that clashed on certain levels, like smooth and fast jazz playing together. Still, there was a connection they could share even though they occupied two completely different worlds.

But Gus knew he could use any connection to build a bridge for communication because he was a negotiator. One of the best.

He kissed his pendant on his way up to the door for good luck. Approaching things this way, he would need more than his fair share of luck. If only the good grace to walk in and out unharmed.

Dr. Jones was a slightly older man but obviously not foolish. Any situation could take a turn for the worst. And he was entering another man's turf. To negotiate.

Gus had brought all his skills with him for his final interview with the only remaining suspect and nothing else. This man had been cleared on paper but not in his mind. He rang the doorbell. A moment later, Dr. Jones answered with a measure of surprise.

"Lieutenant..."

"Gus," Gus said. "Gus is fine."

"Well, Gus," Dr. Jones said. "To what do I owe the pleasure? Please - come on in."

He stepped back and let Gus walk in. Gus checked up and down the street before he entered. No one out watering plants that would watch him. No one in blue jumpsuits working on power lines or sewage to keep tabs on him. Nobody.

Jones glanced up and down the street after Gus passed by. He too saw no one, so he closed the door.

Jones' home was spacious and grand; a custom build villa with jazz that played in every room through speakers in the high corners where the walls met a raised ceiling. The main sitting room, a party-sized walkthrough, had a recessed lounge and fireplace as well as windows facing Toluca Lake without obstruction. It was two whole stories high by itself, with a balcony up top from the second-floor walkway.

"I was about to have a little bite," Jones explained. "Join me for a drink?"

Gus nodded.

He got himself a fixed-up glass courtesy of his host, a nice amber-brown liquid, an expensive, oddball Scotch, named after an old lord, who'd inherited the land it was brewed in, or something to that effect.

It went down smooth and left a satisfying heat on the back of his tongue.

"Sorry for coming by unannounced," Gus said.

"No worries," Jones replied.

He ushered Gus further into his home. Further away from the front door.

They entered a dining room, fitted like a classic club lounge, with pool-table felt on the walls and plush carpeting underneath. They sat across from one another in nice, expensive leather-lined dining seats. Fixtures that fit the psychiatrist to the stars very well.

Everything seemed to be installed to cater to his clients while providing a perfect space for him to relax and chill on his own.

"I won't take up too much of your time," Gus said.

Jones nodded understandingly.

It was time.

"I uh... I just wanted you to know that I know it was you."

Gus then calmly went halfway through his drink while Jones looked at him, perplexed. Gus lifted his glass in Jones' direction as a silent compliment. The Scotch was excellent. He continued.

"Yep. You. Oh, I'm not wearing a wire or anything." He patted himself down, and made it clear his shirt was empty. "Just want to have a light conversation...for now."

Jones nodded and put his drink to the side on a coaster and laced his fingers together on top of the long mahogany table, he at the head of the table and Gus in the first of the other nine chairs.

"Care to elaborate on what we're talking about here?" He asked.

"Yeah. Sure." Gus said.

He put his drink to the side - missed the coaster, then corrected himself - and began.

"The mistake I kept making was going over everything with such a fine-toothed comb. But you knew that about me already. Right?" Gus said.

"Knew what?" Jones replied.

"That I needed my professional mojo back and that I was never going to not fight for my son."

"Admirable quality..." an unsure Jones offered.

Gus could tell things were going to be hard. He was dealing with a brilliant psychiatrist - a psychologist with medical backing. All the

155

willpower of a criminal combined with the guile and understanding of a man trained to master human behavior. He was like him but not like him.

But Gus would remain earnest and steadfast in his approach because that was his way. Just two black men talking, one with power and connections and one without. But Gus knew some things too. Over the last year or so, he'd begun the practice of mentally taking 4,096 people – twelve generations of his ancestors plus the image of his son, into every potentially challenging situation. He knew Dr. Jones had the same number of ancestors, but also knew that he didn't have a child. In his mind... a big advantage for Gus.

And that gave him the conviction to disarm Jones' projection of power, so everyone could feel and be safe.

"Did you know that no survivor from the bank could identify all the other people who went through that same experience?" Gus said.

"Understandable, no? The captors kept us in different rooms. Usually blindfolded... bound." Jones said.

"Yeah," Gus said, feeling a touch of his Scotch. "Looking at the photos, nobody can pick out everybody. But the funny thing? Not one of the other bank customers that day remembered you." Gus said. "Not one."

"That is weird, isn't it?" Jones said, sounding almost offended. "So, nobody remembered me?"

"Not what I said. Several bank employees remembered you but only bank employees, which... I thought was odd. There's no recorded footage for the day of the robbery, but the records center keeps recordings for seven days."

Gus allowed the statement to linger before continuing.

"Did you know that in the six previous days - before the robbery - that you went to the bank seven different times?"

"No. But why is that odd? Some of my clients pay with cash..." Jones said.

"By clients, you mean patients, right?"

Jones made a concessionary nod.

"You're a psychiatrist who treats several Hollywood luminaries, but you cater, largely to psychologists, other psychiatrists..." Gus said.

"Your point?" Jones said.

"Your bank statements for the past year show an average of eight monthly transactions. But the week before the robbery... It's like you tried to plant yourself in their minds before the big day." Gus said.

"That it?" Jones said.

"No," Gus said.

The sauce was hitting, but he also just felt extra saucy. He started to talk with even more confidence, assurance, and procedural basis as he recited the facts of the case he had gathered alone. The polite facts were over. The damning facts began.

"Cathy O'Brien's car seat settings. The bank manager who was killed at the lake? That one." He pointed out at the beautiful body of water at the edge of Jones' property.

Jones knew where Toluca Lake was in relation to where they now sat. He did not flinch; he didn't even blink because he knew exactly where the negotiator-turned-detective was going.

"I'm guessing you parked your car in the bank's lot that morning and waited for Ms. O'Brien. She briefly went inside the bank as the cleaning crew exited. She came out with, what, $50,000 cash - that you later stacked in full view during your robbery? She set the alarm and then drove to the Lake with you in the passenger seat. After her death, you drove her vehicle back to the bank. You wiped everything down for fingerprints but... you never readjusted the driver's seat back to her setting. You left it set for you at 6'-4" and long legs but not for someone 6'-8" with a long upper torso, like Dr. Nolcox."

Gus started to take another sip but decided against it.

"So much was happening that day; I couldn't put my finger on what was wrong because it was right in front of me the whole time. Every one of the victims was shot twice in the heart, but there was no blood splatter. So, they were already dead before you shot 'em. I had a buddy check tissue samples, and sure enough, every one of the deceased had cancer. Terminally. Dr. Nolcox too. Big coincidence."

Dr. Jones poured a bit more drink into his glass to fill it back up. He offered the same to Gus, who held his glass out politely to accept.

An outsider would have assumed the two were concluding a business deal that had benefited both. Totally relaxed.

But Jones realized he'd been caught.

Still, his wrists didn't feel restrained. His heart wasn't burdened. There was no change in the tone between them. In fact, it became even more casual.

"Dr. Nolcox," Jones explained, "specialized in treating the mental and emotional effects terminally ill patients suffer during their... final journey. California is a 'right to die' state. The terminally ill are entitled to voluntarily end their life at a time of their own choosing because, for some, 'dignity' comes into play. Them injecting or ingesting a lethal substance into their own bodies is... their right."

"So," Gus replied, "Dr. Nolcox's little group of cancer patients all decided that voluntary euthanasia was how they wanted to go out?"

"Being united by a cause that hopefully makes the world better for the innocent brings nobility to an unfair and horribly un-noble demise."

Jones' statement hung in the air.

Not a single witness or survivor spoke well of the criminals after the event. They had no idea the robbers were all 'dead people walking' from the moment they woke up that morning. Even online conversations remained firmly quenched in the days after between people discussing the matters that police revealed to the public and the wide, sweeping, unilateral and pure emotional noise of sympathies for the dead. So much sympathy that showing anything else was quickly labeled as hate speech by social media influencers.

"I'd never considered it, but until this," Gus admitted, with a wry smirk, "I didn't know if it was legal or illegal to shoot an already dead body. Turns out it's legal. Laws are funny."

The two then exchanged a couple of 'what if' chess maneuvers.

Jones opened with, "Well, changing the cause of death at this point only robs the families of insurance money and dilutes the power of the message you helped deliver."

"True. But with a tightly written subpoena, I bet we'd discover how and when you picked me." Gus then wondered aloud, "What, you were an expert witness on a case in the same courtroom as me when I was going through one of my hearings?"

Dr. Jones' eyes drifted just slightly to the side. He remembered sitting in the gallery while Theodore Gold did his level best lawyer act and pontificated over the Petitioner's repeated violation of Court Orders and the impact and effect it had on their son and his relationship with Gus Martin, a father, who also happened to be an expert negotiator in the second largest city in America.

Not receiving an answer to what amounted to a rhetorical question simply meant Gus would continue to conduct the business he came for.

"Dr. Nolcox was a patient of yours, and you manipulated this entire situation - which goes against every medical malpractice law there is. That is more than enough reason for me to take you in."

He gently pointed an accusing finger over the rim of his glass at Jones, who took another polite sip of his drink while nodding slightly.

"But you're not going to do that...because you can't." Jones said.

The arrogance was shocking, if not appalling to Gus. Polite company or no, the man had been caught - dead to rights. Gus wasn't expecting a weeping, pleading call for mercy, but he most certainly wasn't expecting the glib, humorless smile that was now on Jones' face.

"Because I can't?" Gus repeated.

Jones shook his head slowly before responding.

"Dr. Nolcox was a good man, a real advocate... and a true ally. He understood that weaponizing his whiteness makes the intention behind "his act" honorable and conversation worthy in the right places. That much-needed change might happen as a result."

Gus noted that Jones did not resort to using air quotes for emphasis. He never did either. Jones continued.

"Right now, "he" is the martyr for a message many needed to hear. His perceived ineptitude for crime will be outweighed by the brilliance of his intention."

This time it was Jones who allowed his commentary to linger as if it were to be savored before he continued.

"Long story short, if you bring charges against me, you'll destroy all the good that's been done because then I'd be the martyr - a black one - and suddenly the intention wouldn't be viewed so nobly. Would it?"

He left Gus stunned at the haughty air of such racially tinged thoughts. A black man pulling the black card on another black man had to be a first.

Jones took another sip, savoring both the drink and the moment.

"Look, what you accomplished lets you write your own ticket. The public sees you as a hero; more importantly, you now have full custody of your son because your case was re-tried in the Court of public opinion before you returned to the Courtroom... But the kicker? The only money that came up missing from the attempted robbery was used to pay off your legal bills."

Gus tried his best to mask a pained expression.

That was the one nagging item he couldn't tie back to the case at all. And now? Here it was, hanging as neatly as a Christmas ornament on a tree Dr. Winston Jones had personally grown.

At first, Gus wanted to believe that Theo Gold had reactivated his case because he was being magnanimous due to Gus' very public heroics at Vista National Bank. Later, when he discovered his bill was current and had a substantial credit, Gus wanted to believe some type of go-fund-me situation had been organized by well-meaning strangers.

But the truth was that he'd been far more interested in seeing his son regularly and in solving this case than digging deeper into finding out who the benevolent strangers might actually be.

Gus had not been interested in finding out about Cathy O'Brien taking money before the bank opened on the day she died or about the cashier's check for his fees being dated two days earlier than the date of the robbery. Had he been interested; he would have investigated to discover who'd fronted the money for the cashier's check and how Cathy O'Brien reimbursed that person via post-dated deposits. Even Sheila's delivering the check to Theo Gold's law firm the day of the robbery could've been discovered had someone – anyone – simply asked the right questions of the right people.

But that hadn't happened.

Now it was time for Gus to once again be, truly authentic. Yes, he could prove he had not stolen money, but he'd have to spend a lot of time and money in Court to do it. Yet again. Further... the original legal fees – as well as the new fees for a new case – would once again become a mountain of unpayable debt.

The 'what if' chess match was now over.

"I see your point," Gus sighed. "Those are bad ingredients for a happy ending."

Jones shrugged nonchalantly.

"But you knew all of that already. You just wanted some closure. Now you have it."

Gus raised his glass.

"Compliments to the chef..."

They sat quietly and quietly took everything in; the victorious negotiator slumped in his chair, feeling the weight of a loss as the criminal mastermind sat across from him. The brilliant black man whose mind had made his singular message become a national discussion off the back of a noble white man who'd already been destined to die.

The villain Jones had created was long buried, and Gus was left to pat down the ground.

"Question," Gus said.

He leaned forward, and his mouth swirled the words around with tension in his lips.

"Why? Why put all of this, your life, your career on the line?"

Jones stared off at the wall behind Gus for a moment, then set his drink down, on the table, with a distinct gavel-like motion.

"Why risk everything?" he asked rhetorically.

He decided to tell Gus a hard truth because he was deserving of that and more.

"Some unicorns are born, but a lot of us are made."

It was at that moment Gus finally realized what it was he'd always seen in Jones' eyes. It was a deeply personal answer he'd given, but without any discernible conflict registering in the windows to his soul. It was the same look he'd seen many times on the job over the years.

He'd seen that same look in the eyes of young Justin Bradley the morning of the bank job.

People with those eyes often stood in broad daylight in front of unsuspecting innocents who could never imagine the darkness those eyes have seen and experienced.

Gus accepted what was, nodded his understanding and silently took his leave, with his drink unfinished.

Jones followed and walked him out. Even held the door for him to go.

Exhausted by years of mental anguish he'd kept locked away, Jones exhaled and subconsciously granted Gus a glimpse that allowed his true self to be fully seen through those eyes.

At that moment, Gus saw the true depth of his darkness, but he also saw his light.

Jones realized what Gus had seen just before he wordlessly closed the door. Then he walked, glass still in hand, to his reclining chair to sit and to think.

He turned up the jazz with a remote, and thought about the day he chose to believe, while a mother and father had argued beyond the walls, about who left whom, who beat whom, and why and, finally, who deserved custody of their child... and who did not.

And how two gunshots, one for each combatant, had quieted the argument forever.

All of which was seen through the slats of an off-white synthetic wood door by a young, frightened Black boy who would later be labelled hyper-sensitive and hyper-aware... because those became his defense mechanisms against those parts of the world that continued to cause him pain.

Winston Jones had been that boy, hiding in the shadows of the apartment's hall closet.

Orphaned, bounced through the System and the homes of barely acquainted relatives, he saw how similar common circumstances begat many but few like him. He saw how the wide array of abuses, depression, anxieties, lies, confusion, anger and fear affected others... both younger and older than he.

His heightened sensitivity recognized the pain and anguish absorbed and exhibited by the young, the small and/or the defenseless. As he himself grew older, he learned to hide inside of his mind so that no matter what was happening to his body, his essence – his soul was always protected. And that part of him always believed or insisted that things should, could and *would* be different than what they were if he could just get old enough, big enough and smart enough.

He held on to that belief for an entire lifetime because it was, truly, all he had. He intuitively had always known that what happened to him had happened for him – whether he liked it or not.

Dr. Winston Jones allowed a tear to fall down his cheek as he stared out into the in-between.

He was, by no means 'free' - but hearing the rumble of an engine in the distance as Gus Martin's new Mustang thrummed down the quiet, picture-perfect street, sounding like a whole stampede of galloping hooves - brought him an unexpected and very welcome emotional release.

He could feel Gus' newfound freedom, and, at this moment, that was enough.

His new belief was that the ripple The Unicorn had created would, in fact, become a wave – if enough people realized that using children to hurt others harmed their children far more than their target.

If more people understood that, then they'd be unicorns too.

Chapter 20

G us returned to his still-like-new apartment in Santa Monica. An elevated homestead with a view of the ocean in the distance, beyond the city lights. A multi-room place was set for a family, and that family was present.

He moved through the living room. Not quite a Jones Manor special but a nice place to stay, with one little corner acting as his office, which he knew, now, he had to tear down and clear out. Then past the kitchen, where he was slowly learning how not to burn things, with one pan still soaking in the sink.

Then, before his bedroom, which was stark and spartan for quick and full rests between future consulting jobs and television interviews, he stopped by Jaylen's room.

It was the best bedroom a now four-year-old could ask for.

Everything he wanted was in it, including things he brought from his mom and stepdad's house. This was his room now. His home. His and his dad's, and he was never happier. The social workers confirmed it over and over. His demeanor was completely different, and for the better now that he was with his daddy... Gus.

The babysitter was gone, and Jaylen was already in his bed with the covers kicked around his feet, just to make a bigger mess for his dad to fix when he got tucked in.

Gus walked over and knelt.

"Go potty and wash your face?" Gus asked.

"Yes," Jaylen giggled.

"Put on lotion, or you trying to be ashy?" Gus said.

Jaylen burst out laughing again while Gus tucked him in.

"Alright. I don't want any foolishness out of you." Gus said.

"I'm not no foolishness," Jaylen replied.

They both laughed from the inside before Gus leaned his head down a bit.

"Ready?" Gus said.

Jaylen nodded, and Gus spoke with a rhythmic cadence Jaylen liked because it made him feel comfortable.

"Now I lay us down to sleep; we pray the lord our souls to keep, the angels watch us through the night, and in the day because it's right. Amen."

"Amen," Jaylen repeated.

Gus leaned down and kissed his son on the forehead.

"'Night, big man," Gus said.

"'Night, Daddy. Um, can you leave the door cracked?"

"Yep," Gus said. "I'll be in to check on you later, okay?"

"'Kay," Jaylen said.

Gus turned the lights down with a dimmer until they were off and left the door ajar just enough so it could let some hall light in.

He was almost out of the doorway, when he turned and opened it again, so the light spilled across Jaylen's waiting face.

"Jaylen... you believe in unicorns?" Gus said.

"Unicorns?" Jaylen asked.

He wondered if it was a trick question but answered honestly just the same.

"Yes, sir. I do." Jaylen said.

Gus smiled.

"Good. Me too. 'Night." Gus said.

Gus took one more glance and then slipped into the hall.

Jaylen nestled into the warmth of his sheets and blanket before glancing down at the middle of his bed. It was a bit dark, still bright enough to keep him comfortable, but he could plainly see the unicorn shape upside down on his blanket. His daddy had it crocheted there to keep him safe at night. And he was glad the unicorn was there, along with his daddy.

He had two guardians to protect him from the darkness...

Epilogue

2:22 pm, and there was so much to be grateful for.

Lynn Kennedy, the LAPD's first female Chief of Police and Black woman, no less, having been in her position just over 90 days, was taking a long weekend to exhale in the sun and near the sand in Costa Rica... with her small inner circle of 'thick as thieves' girlfriends.

Her three friends wanted to get into the Pacific Ocean waters, and that's exactly where they were. Lynn just needed to be near it to hear the centering rhythm and smell the fresh salty sea air in the relative privacy of this decidedly un-touristy beach.

The last couple of months had been a 'trip,' to say the least. So much so that Drew suggested she take one because he's sensitive, very attentive to her needs and likely wanted a couple of days with the fellas.

"He ain't slick." She thought with a giggle.

Thinking of things from where she thought his perspective might be, she figured it had to be tough for him sometimes. They'd moved to Los Angeles a little over three months prior, and for the last two months, there wasn't a day that "Commissioner Evelyn Kennedy" hadn't been in the news, on the news, or discussing the decisions made that day in interviews and even on a couple of the late-night talk shows.

Alone and away from it all, she could admit to herself, with a humility that wasn't necessary for an audience of one, that she'd... navigated the waters of public relations reasonably well. Actually... quite well... truth be told.

Staring out at the beautiful, crystal clear light turquoise water that gradually became a deep, rich, and velvety blue the further away from shore one looked, she sighed and accepted that she'd won a place at the table.

She was the LAPD's first 'this' and 'that'; for now, she'd become somewhat of a celebrity – which is a tricky, finicky business. She patently refused to accept all of the credit, deferring instead to the mayor's imaginary wisdom, the entire team of the LAPD, who, frankly, truly needed some good P.R. for a change, and, of course, the astonishingly heroic Lt. Augustus Martin.

Now, here she was. Firmly implanted as the Chief of Police when most had figured she'd never last a year.

Heady stuff, indeed. But she saw how people now gravitated to her when they were out in public together and how Drew would, figuratively speaking, be pushed aside unless she made a conscious effort to make sure he was included in her new reality – now their new reality.

She knew that they were 'okay' and that he was genuinely proud of her accomplishments, but there was an imbalance that had been introduced that neither was expecting and, as her best friend *and* husband would say from time to time, "Little things become big things if you don't catch 'em early."

It was those comments, said allegedly in jest, that stuck with her because she felt a subtext underneath his ever-present smile. The dramatic encounter with The Unicorn had ripped open deep, personal scar tissue that slowly and insidiously eased into their home, causing some very tough conversations between her and Drew. So much so, that they'd returned to couple's counseling for the first time in several years.

The issues The Unicorn raised in such a shocking fashion caused the two to reopen less-than-pleasant aspects of their individual histories. She'd always been honest and upfront about her inability to have children due to her history of Endometriosis and the repeated surgical removal of scar tissue that eventually forced her to decide between horrific menstrual cycles or freedom from the pain.

The reality of her situation had been soothed by her own eventual acceptance of what was and that there was a reason for everything and all the self-comforting platitudes one programs their mind with to first survive the horror before accepting that the ghosts of a decision are far better than trying to live with the alternative.

Plus, Drew had always maintained that he'd never wanted to have children, so Lynn had always taken him at his word. But Drew, like everyone else, had watched everything via social media and later television that day. He couldn't possibly have avoided it if he'd wanted to. Everyone at his firm knew exactly who his wife was and what she did professionally.

Watching Gus expose the realities of his personal life to save those hostages almost made Drew sick to his stomach at several junctures along the way. He'd shared that with Lynn after-the-fact. But when it was brought up in therapy, and he was asked to dig deeper to find out why Gus's situation had affected him so, he responded to the therapist's skilled prodding with a shocked Lynn sitting to his immediate right.

It wasn't that he hadn't wanted children. It was because he never wanted to risk the possibility of a child of his experiencing what he'd gone through growing up in the same home as his father.

Hiding from trauma brought about by generational curses is not the same as healing from it. Not by a long shot.

Of course, Lynn felt his pain as she'd watched a grown man, *her* man, sob so hard he physically shook. But part of her also felt repulsed because maybe, just maybe, part of him wanted to be with someone who could never change their mind or entertain the possibility of bringing a child into his life based on a choice he couldn't control.

Indeed. They were putting in the work because 'love' is active and evolving. Of course, they were aiming for 'forever,' but forever wasn't always going to be easy.

She realized she'd been rambling in her brain because, just maybe... she *was* buzzed.

She'd never risk being "wildly intoxicated" – not here in Tamarindo or even if she were in L.A. with Drew. She had too much to lose to be frivolous. But she took another sip of her blended Cadillac margarita sans salt because she *was* 'nice,' and she wanted to keep her vibe right where it was.

The mind mess had lessened a great deal; this was only their third day in paradise. Still, there were elements of the situation with The Unicorn she could now disassemble and examine to her satisfaction without the glare of the media spotlight. Nor did she need to be politically correct.

Her starting place was that 'wrong' had been done, but 'right' was the result.

Commissions were established to examine how things are handled in Family Court at the state and Federal levels. How kids were seen and protected in court proceedings was now a 'hot' issue, which made it election campaign fodder, but the change would take place, however incrementally.

Dr. Lorenzo Nolcox and his failed bank heist turned 'cause of the century,' as the media referred to it, from two months before, had been her ticket to perceived legitimacy - if not outright acceptance - among the rank and file.

Further, she'd honored her word to Gus about personally watching out for his best interests. Granted, the circumstances she'd created seemed unnecessarily awkward and uncomfortable to and for him. But she knew he'd never let the case go until he'd gotten to the bottom of things to find the truth; he needed to be free from all that had happened before. So, by suspending him with pay, she put Gus in a position to do exactly that while keeping his findings away from the spotlight's glare.

She knew that Gus had been 'right' about the late Dr. Nolcox not being the man most responsible for the mission The Unicorn had undertaken that day. She wasn't positive who the real culprit had been, but if she were a betting woman – which she wasn't – she'd put all her money on Dr. Winston Jones.

A woman in her position had access to practically all records kept on almost every legal citizen in the United States. Whether their records were sealed or not was of no consequence. So, after narrowing her list of potential subjects, Lynn Kennedy settled on him because not only did he fit the profile Gus so accurately rattled off to her in the thick of battle, his records from when he was a minor reflected an ugliness that would break the great majority of people... and those few who survived similar experiences will be affected for a lifetime and likely seen as 'odd' by "regular people."

The importance of the issue that had been raised and exposed by The Unicorn could not be overstated; she, too, had grown up affected by the battle. But not bringing the person most responsible to Justice required an outlook she was unaware she could accept before this circumstance.

While she was a youngster and before he passed, her father would remind her that there was 'right,' there was 'wrong,' but what was 'best' always needed to be considered. It explained why he hadn't come around as often as either of them would've liked. He knew the torment his daughter would experience when she returned to her mother's care, "smiling too much" or "looking just like your daddy" after being with him. He eventually stayed away to protect her from wrath aimed at those parts of his daughter that reminded certain people of him.

He wasn't equipped to win an unending battle with no rules... where the only casualties from their bi-weekly weekend visits would always be Lynn and himself. So, to save his daughter, he took on twice the pain by simply not showing up. But, in his mind, that was the only course of action he could take, legally, that would protect her.

As he couldn't articulate his decision to one so young, she was left to simply feel both guilty and abandoned. Feelings confirmed regularly and repeatedly by the unpredictability of his absences. Her guilt stemmed from those times when she'd reported and even stolen things from her father's apartment as she'd been encouraged to do by her mother. She'd been told she was "only helping Mommy" but she carried the burden of pleasing one parent by harming the other – which harmed her. She'd been repeatedly told about her father's cheating and other shortcomings being the reasons for their separation, so she simply wanted to fix the sadness and anger that was used to manipulate her... but never could.

Only once had her father asked about some missing paperwork, and she lied about ever having seen it. He'd never asked Lynn about those types of things again, but she knew in her heart that he was likely aware of who'd removed it.

Yes, part of her saw the wrong, but she also recognized what was best for many of the most vulnerable participants in the dance of Family Court proceedings across America, certainly, but the dynamic was not relegated to the U.S. alone. Consequently, her choices consisted of; doing what was 'right' and being the reason defenseless children lost a hope they didn't know they had; putting Gus back into the Court System for something he didn't do; potentially losing a trial after indicting Jones, another Black man, for his unconventional attempt to demand positive change for a System with inconsistent empathy. Sure, she was almost sure they could nail him for kidnapping, but that might be the only charge that might stick after a public opinion and media shitstorm. She wasn't even certain of that, though. Where would they find potential members for a jury who hadn't seen or heard of what The Unicorn had done? Further, how could she guarantee a conviction against a man attempting to save all children of all races - from broken homes or those with single parents, who ended their relationships acrimoniously?

A different option included several of the same elements but would end up making Gus look like the bad guy and Jones, the good guy, but the momentum Jones created would be lost because of built-in, ongoing societal prejudice that would either never be seriously addressed or the discussion would never last long enough to affect anything.

This left option number three, which was to risk allowing herself to be found or labelled 'incompetent,' which was already on the table when she first accepted the position. Because, of course, it was. But short of that happening, the decision she made was the only option in her multilevel chess game that allowed children everywhere, Gus, Jones, *and* herself, to all 'win' – even though they would be the only three people in the entire world who knew of their collective victory.

So, this was why her life had taken the turns it had. Why she'd had the parents she did and why her mother's demands on Lynn were designed solely to make her mom look good to those she wanted to impress or be accepted by - but never was. There was no love. Just the mimicking of behaviors others unconsciously displayed as they exhibited or demonstrated physical characteristics of what appeared to be love. At that moment, Lynn accepted that she'd needed every bit of pain and disappointment she'd ever experienced to force herself to learn how to manage people and assess many things simultaneously. She needed those skills to survive her environment – because that was her set of defense mechanisms.

Evelyn 'Lynn' Kennedy learned to play three-dimensional chess and view the world through a kaleidoscope so she could measure, manipulate, and affect the amount of pain she would experience or cause.

In that moment, she realized one could have a good life despite one's parents or a bad one because of them, but you have to make a choice, and you can only do so when you've become aware that a choice exists.

She knew how special a man she had in Drew. He was a rarity among men of color because he'd sought therapy to rid himself of familial curses and demons before they'd even met. Clearly the work had not yet been completed but he always believed everything he'd experienced, through years of his father's numerous abuses, prepared him to be ready for a woman equally yoked but not in a traditional sense.

Even though Drew is an architect, Lynn was still the major breadwinner. But for them, the journey wasn't about the money. It was about being the best versions of themselves for themselves and each other. It was about the ride and the positive imprint they each hoped to leave behind, individually and as a couple.

She suddenly needed to take a bigger sip of the margarita because the needle was either going a little deeper than before or the artist was repeatedly hitting a susceptible area.

Although far outside of her day-to-day personality, this was something she needed to do for herself. Nobody would ever see it other than Drew because it was so high up and because it wasn't very large. But it would be a forever reminder of the very exclusive club she now belonged to and that she would never leave.

The pinching, vibrating pain she felt was because every single bit of one specific area had to be pierced repeatedly to give the rendering the distinctive characteristic that allowed privileged eyes to recognize what it truly was.

Taking in the beauty of the shimmering blue-green water through the window while lying on the table, Lynn knew that she and Dr. Winston Jones' paths *would* eventually cross again. She also knew that she and Lieutenant Augustus 'Gus' Martin, one way or another, had many more dragons to slay. Perhaps even working together to do it while trusting and believing in one another.

"So much mind mess to work through and prioritize," she thought. It might take a few years, but she realized that, perhaps, it was time to put 'Mayor of Los Angeles' on her list and begin strategizing.

"To whom much is given..." she said aloud to no one in particular. The tattoo artist grunted a semi-acknowledgment and continued her work. Lynn Kennedy took another sip and smiled while happy tears formed in her eyes.

Despite her path, her journey of healing had rewarded her with a genuine love – not of the storybook variety but a love worthy of the work involved. More importantly, it was a love that loved her back. She was accepted and revered for who she was in the present with a mutual allowance of space to breathe and grow into ever higher versions of herself. Indeed, she'd learned to love herself through challenges and triumphs because ups and downs were a part of life. 'Perfection' could, on occasion, be obtained but expecting herself to maintain it was neither healthy nor realistic. Learning to have compassion for herself balanced the compassion and concern she had for the well-being of others. It was a gift that she had worked extremely hard for and had absolutely, positively earned.

She was a wife and a fierce warrior who chose to use her powers for good... or at least for what was best.

"Unicorns rise up." She whispered.

And she was right.

D. ELLIOT WOODS

ACKNOWLEDGEMENTS

I am very grateful to be surrounded by folks who truly want to see other people win in this game called 'Life', beginning with my two lovely, brilliant sisters Aubaine & Carrie, my mom, the great and wise 'Nana-Betts,' who's love and belief in me has never, ever wavered, my man Robb Armstrong who jumped in with both feet to design the book cover for "RISE OF THE UNICORN" and who also wrote a special and heartfelt foreword. * dap * Trust me when I tell you, Robb is a rare breed in Hollywood. To my forever friend, Tiffany Hofer, a miraculous combination of angel, warrior and amazingly insightful mom. To Patrick H. Johnson and Ian Wenger, good dudes, great friends and fantastic dads who 'held the line' over the years. The whole, entire DeFrantz family (LOL), y'all mean the world to me. To my family and friends – from Indianapolis to Denver & Colorado Springs to Bermuda and Smyrna, TN, I so appreciate your love and support. And finally, to the many teachers and coaches along the way who either helped or FORCED (LOL) me to grow. Mr. Howard Parks at Julian D. Coleman Academy (formerly # 110) in Indy, Mrs. Graves at Tech and Coach Don Thomas at Shortridge, the always encouraging Dr. Ellen Rosenthal at The Colorado College, legendary actress and tremendously supportive, Alfre Woodard and iconic actor/director Bill Duke have all had a tremendous impact when it was most needed.

Lastly, I'd like to thank YOU for 'rolling the dice' on this book. I hope you enjoyed the characters, their story and that it's helped to make you think and feel the need for significant change. Tell your friends so we can turn this story into a major motion picture and help start a conversation or movement with a larger audience.

Even when you're in the darkness, never, EVER be afraid to shine your light. DEW

ABOUT THE AUTHOR

D. Elliot Woods has been an LA-based Film, TV and Commercial Actor for more than 25 years. From human and alien roles across various Star Trek films and TV shows to appearances on LOOT, NCIS: LA, HBO's Ballers, Marvel's Agents of S.H.I.E.L.D, Friends, Drake & Josh as well as over 100 commercials for numerous household brands. His extensive industry experience and knowledge bleeds through into his writing. His Fly Free Entertainment production banner is dedicated to producing his own projects as well as helping train a whole new generation of creatives.

D. Elliot resides in LA and strives to teach his children that anything is possible. He pours all his knowledge of the industry into writing captivating stories featuring diverse, non-stereotypical characters. His unique way of viewing the world elevates his writing to thought-provoking, heart-wrenching, emotional and even comedic, in a fresh way that readers and audiences will fall in love with. When he's not writing or acting, he loves to cheer for his kids in everything they do, watch men's and women's basketball, travel, listen to Jazz, and enjoy delicacies from all over the world. Of course, he also has his hands full with his Siberian Husky, who pretends to be deaf and won't help type, but has a black belt in playtime. Woods hopes to remind us all to cherish the little moments because eventually, we'll look back and realize that they all happened for you.

- Dani

@UnicornsRiseUp on FB, Twitter and IG

@FlyFreeEnt1 on FB, Twitter and IG

About the Publisher

Founded by actor, writer, VO artist and author D. Elliot Woods, Fly Free Entertainment, Inc is an imaginative content studio and production company headquartered in Burbank, California. We primarily specialize in writing, voice over and the creation of scripted and unscripted content for large and small screens as well as the occasional novel.